The Love - Adept

By the same Author

★

Novels

POOR CLARE
THE BETRAYAL
THE BRICKFIELD
FACIAL JUSTICE
THE HIRELING
A PERFECT WOMAN
THE GO-BETWEEN
MY FELLOW DEVILS
THE BOAT
EUSTACE AND HILDA
THE SIXTH HEAVEN
THE SHRIMP AND THE ANEMONE
SIMONETTA PERKINS

Short Stories

TWO FOR THE RIVER
THE WHITE WAND
THE TRAVELLING GRAVE
THE KILLING BOTTLE
NIGHT FEARS
THE COLLECTED SHORT STORIES OF L. P. HARTLEY

Literary Criticism
THE NOVELIST'S RESPONSIBILITY

L. P. HARTLEY

The Love-Adept

A VARIATION ON A THEME

On a poet's lips I slept
Dreaming like a love-adept
In the sound his breathing kept
                    SHELLEY

HAMISH HAMILTON
LONDON

First published in Great Britain, 1969
by Hamish Hamilton, Ltd
90 Great Russell Street, London WC1
Copyright © 1969 by L. P. Hartley
SBN 241 01737 8
Printed in Great Britain by
Cox & Wyman Limited, London, Fakenham and Reading

James Golightly was nearing the end of his novel. The five main characters – well, seven if you counted Jock's two children – made a sort of frieze before his mental eye, a moving frieze like a caravan in the desert in which some overtook others and then in their turn dropped back, although the children always came last. They were not characters in search of an author; James had authorized them, in both senses of the word. He had brought them to life, or so he thought; now he must decide what to do with them, to decide how they should make their exits – not necessarily from life, but from their lives which he had tried to conjure up in the reader's imagination.

Pauline the actress, approaching middle-age (how old was middle age?) Alexey, her devoted swain, who wanted nothing more, and nothing better, than to put his considerable worldly goods at her disposal; Jock, the good-looking chauffeur, to whom she accorded favours she did not accord Alexey, although he paid for them; Mrs. Kirkwood, the guardian and foster-mother of Jock's children, for whose keep Alexey indirectly paid; and Gina, their mother, Jock's wife, who had abandoned him for a Negro lover.

Was it a subject for tragedy? James asked himself. He had never written a novel that ended happily; he had been taught to think that a novel with a happy ending was inferior, as a work of art, to a novel that ended 'badly' – as did many of the greater and more highly esteemed novels of the past. How

1

much superior, for instance, were the novels of Thomas Hardy that ended 'badly' to those that ended 'well'.

There were exceptions, of course. Jane Austen was one of the most eminent. 'Let other pens dwell on grief and misery,' she declared, 'I quit those odious subjects as soon as I can.' But, thought James, in spite of the Napoleonic War, it was easier then to think of people 'living happily ever after'. In these days people were not expected, and did not themselves expect, to live happily now, and certainly not ever after. The twentieth century with its world wars that had killed so many men had also killed the notion of perpetual and even temporary happiness.

'Oh dear,' thought James, 'what shall I do? I don't want to add to the sum of human misery even in the pages of a novel. All the same I cannot let my characters get off scot-free. I don't feel that Pauline and Jock, who had behaved quite badly, and Gina who had behaved very badly, and Mrs. Kirkwood who was extremely grasping, and even Alexey who was more sinned against than sinning – but he was such a *fool* – I don't feel they should be let off with a caution. On the other hand they aren't the raw material of tragedy, they lack the stature, personal, moral, or emotional, to warrant them murdering each other, though we read in the papers almost daily of lesser people than they who do!'

What would Elizabeth think about it, and what would the other three Elizabeths, who were also his friends, by a coincidence, think about it? Elizabeth was a common name: James's own mother had been called Elizabeth, which was perhaps why he had a pro-Elizabethan bias and why his age (he was rising fifty) had been for many years the Elizabethan Age.

He had great respect for women's judgment, in artistic matters, at any rate. They judged immediately, by their own feelings; they had an instinctive aesthetic response. They were not overawed by resounding names, or contemptuous of obscure ones. They were not like men, who had to consult other men, or learned works about standards of literature, before they could give an opinion. Nor were they, as some male critics are, intent on showing, sometimes by showing off, how little or how much a book has affected them personally, and their mood of the moment.

In common with many authors, James wrote with certain people, fit but few, in mind. He wrote as it were *for* them, and did his best work when he was most *en rapport* with them. In some mysterious way, some form of thought-transference such as birds have, they influenced the whole flock; they acted as his intermediaries with the public. Left wheel! Right wheel! Invisibly present, listening to his thoughts, they put him in touch with himself, and through himself with the public; and although it is not necessarily good for an author to be himself (oh the ambiguity of this phrase! Good for him? Good in the slang sense, 'Good for you', or good in a general way?). But it was certainly better to be himself than anyone else.

'Dear, dearest Elizabeth, how do you think this novel ought to end? I have almost decided *not* to make it end in tragedy, because I haven't the guns for that and I'm not sure you would like it, even if I had – you don't really *believe* in tragedy, do you? Either Pauline or Alexey or Jock would have ample excuse in the eyes of the law as at present constituted to murder each other. They could all, with the approval of the permissive society, plead that they were suffering from "diminished responsibility", as indeed they were. They all had something vital to lose, and Gina (I forgot to mention her), if she wasn't a natural murderess was a natural murderee; I myself could hardly keep my fingers off her, if you know what I mean.

A*

3

'In one way and another they were all in danger, and the stage is set for tragedy, but could I bring it off? What do you think, dear Elizabeth?'

'Well, as usual, James, you haven't given me enough to go on.'

'I know, Elizabeth, I know, and *you* know why. If I told you more I should lose interest in the tale. It has to be my secret, just as a bird's nest has to be the secret of the mother-bird; if some one so much as looks at the eggs, let alone touches them, she is apt to desert. But couldn't you, just from the little I have told you, write your thoughts to mine and fertilize them? If I knew your thoughts were with me, it would be a sort of inspiration to me, and things would become possible that now seem impossible to my flagging muse. *You* are my Muse, dearest Elizabeth; you create the state of mind in which *I* can create! You relieve the surface irritation of my mind far better than a drink would – an alcoholic drink, I mean. You are my Pierian spring!' –

'Well, I'll do my best, James. I'll do my best.'

The second Elizabeth replied in much the same strain, and James was making headway when unwisely he summoned to his aid the shade of the third Elizabeth, and his pen came to a grinding halt. Hostile influences seemed to flow around and make nonsense of everything he had written, was writing, and was going to write. He laid down his pen. He must have offended her, but how? 'Go away, go away,' he mentally cried, trying to banish her into the circumambient aether. 'You are a witch!' And after a while it did seem as though he had succeeded in exorcising her. Haltingly his pen began to move again, gaining pace as if spurred on by the visitation of the fourth Elizabeth, the Elizabeth whose friendship and whose opinion he valued most, and the only one of the quartet who could sometimes make her voice audible as well as her presence

4

felt. With pen poised he waited, almost as a mystic might await a vision; but not a sound, not even a sensation; the line of communication between them was dead.

Sadly he laid down his pen – he always wrote in long-hand – and mused on his musings. Two Elizabeths seemed each to have contributed their quota of suggestions. But was it they, or was it he himself, projecting himself into their personalities, who had thought up these divergent views of how the 'Love-Adept' should end? He tried to envisage in turn the appearance of each Elizabeth. Their looks were as diverse as their opinions might be (when they had given him their opinions) and each held in her hand a mirror reflecting his own face. He had been talking to himself; but an objective view-point, several objective view-points, not in line with his own, had entered in.

It was the Elizabeths he wanted most to please, and through them his readers, all of whom, in one way or another they represented. He couldn't reach his readers unless he first reached them; they were his touchstones of readability. If they weren't interested in the book, covering as they did such a wide bracket of human sympathy, nobody would be.

An author can only reach his public via the interest, increasing snowball-wise, of a few like-minded people – in his case, the Elizabeths.

The Elizabeth whose opinion, favourable or unfavourable, helpful or unhelpful, he set the most store by, had abstained from the conference. She would not come at his call; she remained obstinately silent. Why? The third Elizabeth had shown her disapproval plainly enough.

The others had said their say. Whether it was what they would really have said, or what he would have liked them or not liked them to say, he couldn't tell. Who can tell, in an imaginary conversation with a friend, what his or her replies will be? He might have got the Elizabeths who seemed to have spoken to him, quite wrong.

'Comme la vie est difficile, comme la vie est dure!'

.   .   .

James hadn't yet decided on the ending, but he hoped it would surprise them all. If the book did come out, he would send them each a pre-publication copy, and each copy, he thought confusedly, for by now he had got the names mixed up in his mind, should be dedicated to 'Elizabeth' – the individual Elizabeth and the collective Elizabeths to whom he owed so much, but especially to the fourth Elizabeth, from whom, alas, he had received no psychic message.

CHAPTER I

Flat 119,
Montcalm House,
The Heights of Abraham,
Quebec.

Dear James,

First of all let me thank you very, very much for giving me a copy of your latest, but I hope not your last, novel 'The Love-Adept'. And thank you still more (for there are degrees of gratitude, as of most other emotions) for dedicating it to me. I am quite overwhelmed. No one, I am sure, has ever thought of dedicating a book to me before, or still less, done it. As some-one said, 'I shall go down to posterity on the hem of your garment.' I never expected to go down to posterity at all, but I couldn't wish for a better way.

Does this sound too impersonal and too *literary*, dear James? I hope not. But in writing to a writer one has to try to be literary, or at any way, literate! It is a sort of challenge! If I was talking to you, I should, as they say, 'express myself differently'. I wish I was talking to you, and I wish it wasn't so long since we talked to each other. We talked to each other a great deal at one time, didn't we? Before I got married and went to Canada? I'm afraid (I may be flattering myself but how can I not be flattered after receiving the honour of your dedication? I simply *bask* in it) – I'm afraid, I was going to say, that you were somehow hurt when I married Frank. At the time it seemed inevitable – he carried me off my feet. It doesn't seem so inevitable now, but I won't go into that. We all make mistakes, and at any rate I have stuck to mine, just as the hero of your novel (in a very different way) seems to have stuck to his. The only way of dealing with mistakes is to stick to them; that way, you keep your dignity and your pride, and there is a general face-saving. I haven't much face to save – I doubt if you would recognize me after these years, and I ask myself, would James have dedicated this book to me if he saw me now? I doubt it, but you were always a faithful soul (no insult intended!).

But poor Alexey! You were quite right to give him a foreign name (derived, I think you said, from his foreign ancestry) for no true Englishman would have behaved as he did. The average Englishman's romantic feelings soon peter out, as I have cause to know. Alexey was carried off his feet from the first moment when he met Pauline, and they never touched the ground until they began to feel the earth and drag a bit, as an aeroplane does when it touches down. That is the dangerous moment; it happened to me much sooner than it happened to Alexey. He fed on his dreams (his dream, I should say) whereas I had to feed on reality, a much less appetizing feast, and feed my children too, *and* my husband, who is still very choosy about his food.

Poor Alexey – I say again. What a dance Pauline led him – horrid girl! There are moments in your novel when I would gladly strangle her. He followed her about like a dog, bitch that she was. But it was like following Cupid for his loaves and fishes. He got nothing out of her – at least I think not – in return for the devotion he gave her. He wasn't a rich man, although he had enough to live on, enough to make him independent of her, and her dependent on him. And those letters he wrote her nearly every day – surely they would have melted a heart of *stone*. Most of the best love-letters we know of have been written by women – Lady Bessborough, Mlle. de Lespinasse, and the Portuguese Nun, whoever she was. Men aren't so good at them – they are too self conscious I suppose, and besides that, they are afraid of giving themselves away. It's the business-instinct – nothing on paper. Frank was hopeless at it. You couldn't tell from his letters that he was ever in love with me: perhaps he never was. He relied on his looks, and on his manner, and the fact, which is, or seems to be, so supporting to a man, that other men took him at his own valuation.

But I am wandering from *The Love-Adept* and all the pleasure it gave me – sad as that pleasure is. Not really wandering, though; the point I wanted to make was, how beastly of that hateful Pauline to have ignored Alexey's letters or only answered one in ten, when she happened to feel like it. It is true she had her work cut out, going up and down the country, in repertory companies and sometimes on the stage in London, and occasionally in T.V., but you make it clear that she wasn't a *really* good actress; she was often *resting* when she must have had plenty of time on her hands – time enough to take up a pen and write. It is true, too, that she had that shadowy and rather shady lover, the chauffeur, whom she sometimes called her husband, and his two children, for whom she pretended to feel responsible, although they weren't hers.

How all this was managed isn't quite clear. I suppose that you, as a bachelor (but why? but why?) wouldn't know how the married, or half-married, part of the world lives. Husbands, or lovers, are not just like pawns in a game, nor are children. They aren't a children's game, compèred by a sugar-daddy either, they penetrate into reality, they *constitute* reality, I might say – at least they have, in my case. And there isn't much beauty in having children, they're a chore, really, certainly not the kind of beauty that Alexey found in the mere idea of Pauline.

You give her the effect of beauty; but why didn't she

9

respond to the beauty in Alexey's heart (you never said he was good-looking)? Instead she preferred this taxi-driver or whatever he was (you didn't make that quite clear) with his thews and sinews, and his hairy cheeks that blunted the razor, his eight-inch wrists, and his everlasting harping upon *money* – to poor Alexey, who never gave a thought to money, and who had every quality, especially idealism, that a woman most needs.

At least I do, and I had it with you, during our too brief friendship.

Was it my fault that our friendship was too brief? I fear it was; and yet if you had taken a stronger line – not a strong line, for that isn't in your character – but a definite line, a line I could have caught hold of and held on to – things might have been different. Happier for me, certainly, and perhaps – who knows? – happier for you. You could have dedicated yourself to me, instead of a book. How silly that sounds – but I should certainly have dedicated myself to you.

Now there are all sorts of questions that I want to ask you, and all sorts of characters besides Alexey and Pauline and her regrettable attendant that I should like to discuss. You have put more people into this book than you usually do, haven't you? As a rule they (your books) are rather sparsely furnished (what a dreadful expression!) – with human material, I mean. You once told me that your novels were about two people, man and woman, man and man, woman and woman, with rival and conflicting egoisms, each intent on interpenetration but each really loathing the idea of it. These unfortunate couples (if you can call characters so disjointed a couple) were, you said, surrounded by a host of shadowy witnesses, leading more or less normal lives, never fully characterized, but making a sort of chorus or environment to the two chief sufferers. You said that this wasn't as unreal as it sounds, because most people – or most people whom it interested you to write about – live in a vacuum *à deux*, or even in a vacuum *tout seul*, and the others are like one's fellow-spectators at a theatre, necessary to make a tolerably full house, but not more important to oneself, or one's two selves than the people one barges into, who always look rather cross, on one's way to taking one's seat, or seats.

I'm sure you said something like this, didn't you? You see what a good memory I have!

In a way it is the same with *The Love-Adept*, Alexey is isolated by his obsession with Pauline; Pauline, despite her commitment to the egregious but physically fascinating Jock, and his children, is isolated – against her will? – by the strength of Alexey's obsession for her. She cannot bring herself to throw in her lot with him, marriage-wise, because of these commitments wretched creature that she is, although he is worth all the rest of them put together.

But you *have* individualized some of the characters – Jock sticks out like a sore thumb, and the children have each their little parts to play, and it is a pity that Alexey's friend and mentor, Adrian, who was so right to try to make him forget about Pauline, fades out so quickly. Such a voice often fades out, especially when it has been disregarded. But the others seem to me like real people, not just scarecrows, or weathercocks to show which way the wind is blowing.

I said I meant to stick to Frank, and I did mean to, until I read your book, which showed me the folly of sticking to a mistake. In Alexey's case Pauline was a mistake; in my case Frank was. I don't feel so sure now that I *shall* stick to him – he certainly hasn't stuck to *me*, except in the way a limpet sticks. I'm not too old to try again, and much as I enjoy the kindness and geniality of the people out here, I am homesick for England, and the friends I used to have and still have there – you among them. I should studiously avoid you, of course, I shouldn't try to be another Pauline! I shouldn't let you follow me about, and I am sure you wouldn't want to.

What do you think?

A great many people would say I am mad to leave Frank just because of his constant infidelities, his constancy, I might call it, for there is nothing else that he is constant about! He has a way with him, both with men and women, and is very much liked. I feel I am beginning to be regarded as a sour-puss, because I can't take his escapades light-heartedly. Lookers-on see most of the game, because to them it *is* a game, whereas to me, who for six months or so enjoyed Frank's undiluted devotion (and that was something!) it's not a game at all, as any woman, or most women, in my position would tell you. I can't help it, but my mind dwells on the happiness of the past and the bleakness of the future.

We have one child, as you know, and no doubt I should be given 'custody of her' (what a dreadful expression!). She quite likes me, I think; we can discuss clothes and such things together, as all women, whatever their ages, can; but her heart is really with her father – as so many other hearts are! and I don't feel sure she would be happy separated from him, little as he can help her in the way of growing up (she is sixteen now) compared with what I can, or would like to.

When I think of the unswerving devotion of your Alexey to his stupid Pauline (well, not stupid, I suppose, she knew which side her bread was buttered), my blood boils, and I can't help comparing her lot with mine. She took so much, and gave so little. With me it's the other way round. You remember what Jane Austen said, or what Anne Elliot said on her behalf – 'all the privilege I claim for my own sex is that of loving longest when existence, or when hope, is gone'.

I used to applaud that sentiment, and I still think it is true, but no longer want to illustrate it or be ruled by it. Now that I have read your book I realize that even men are capable of constancy, at least in the pages of a novel! So why shouldn't *I* find an Alexey? I should treat him much better than Pauline did – I should cling to him instead of being clung to.

But how silly all this is. The course of fiction is so different from the course of nature, and I can't imagine why I seemed to find a resemblance, or rather a contrast, between Alexey's case and mine. What I really wanted to tell you was how much I enjoyed your book, and how grateful and honoured and flattered I am to have had it dedicated to me. Besides all that, it is a link that has been missing for a long time. Perhaps we could forge another, if I come back to England? But that depends on you – I wasn't joking when I said we must stick to our mistakes, or when I said we *mustn't* stick to them.

With my love and many congratulations on *The Love-Adept* (somehow the two seem to have got mixed up!).

Elizabeth

P.S. This letter is much, much too long, but I couldn't have expressed, or even acknowledged, my debt to you on a single sheet of paper.

P.P.S. I have only got as far as page 110, but then I've only had the book two hours. I'm longing to know how it finishes. I think I can guess, but I may be wrong. The post is quicker, I'm told, between Canada and London than it is between London and London, so I hope it will steal a march on your other fans!

P.P.P.S. Did Alexey have any affairs on the side? I feel he *must* have had; not *in spite* of being so taken up with Pauline, but *because* he was so taken up with her. The fact that she wouldn't accord him her favours which I regard as a point in *her* favour – (let us always be sincere!) must have been a great strain on him, and led to little indulgences which, without Pauline gnawing at his vitals he wouldn't have been tempted to.

CHAPTER II

117 Chillinghurst Court,
S.W.7.

Dearest Elizabeth,

  I am so delighted that you like *The Love-Adept* and I only wish that your letter had been twice the length.

  To begin with my book (as every author would like to!). I'm sorry you found Pauline so unsympathetic: I didn't mean her to be: I meant to strike a mean, a happy mean, between her and Alexey. A moral mean? an emotional mean? How mean the word sounds, applied to human relationships! But there is the golden mean, something to aim at, if we could ever achieve it! A moral balance between two human beings, both of whom, as human beings, have some weight and worth. A large claim, I must admit; but I am no Calvinist, and I think that every soul (what a word to use! would any member of the rising generation understand it? – I'm not at all sure that I understand it myself) . . .We are told that all souls are equal before God. In the spiritual world absolute democracy reigns. 'With respect' (as Stalin used to say in his rather disrespectful war-time communications to the weaker countries, including ours) I don't quite agree. I think that some souls are more worthwhile – whatever 'worthwhile' means – than others. Certainly most people put people they know, and still more, people they don't know, politicians, film-stars and the like – into a kind of hierarchy of ranks, conditions and degrees. Not according to their faults and their virtues – for faults and virtues as criteria

14

are out of date – nor even by their good-looks or their sex-appeal, but by their attractiveness to the feeling of the moment, the contemporary *zeitgeist*, they can be recognized and assessed.

Oh, what a sentence! But you see what I mean. Alexey and Pauline were hopelessly dissimilar characters, but he had the quality of devotion, single-hearted devotion which in my eyes still means something, and she had her career as an actress, a moderately successful actress, her very normal, though un-conventional relationship with Jock, and still, in spite of all these activities, practical and emotional, she tries to find some place in her heart for Alexey and his devouring but probably platonic passion for her.

Did he have little affairs on the side with other women, not quite prostitutes, but nearly, to whom he would have given his affections in a light way, just as, in a light way, his affections could have been returned? It would have made him more human, more in tune with modern taste, and perhaps more pathetic. I wanted him to seem pathetic, and I did give indica-tions that there were moments, when Pauline hasn't answered his daily or twice daily letters for a week or more, that he did contemplate seeking their relief. In fact I hinted, as delicately as I could, that he tried it once or twice. (How difficult it is to say something, and yet not seem to say it!) But I decided that such aberrations would not appease him but only damage 'the image of his immortal love', for he was in love with the image, perhaps more than with the woman, but he could not (in his imagination at any rate) have the one without the other.

I suppose that they each represent only too obviously the rival claims of reality and fantasy, but he would be a bold man or a bold woman who would confidently say which of the two was the greater factor in ordinary human life.

You, my dear, clearly take the view that Pauline was, in the eventual scales, a light-weight compared with Alexey – a bantam-weight or even a feather-weight! – in which, if I may say so, you are guilty of showing the prejudice that women are accused of having against women. Being a man I cannot quarrel with you, even if I wanted to, but I think that in this case you are unjust. Pauline had a myriad claims of life pressing upon her. Making a career was one, and earning a living from it was another. Jock, for all his good looks and his motoring activities – and the prestige and convenience they brought her, was a financial liability, as he liked to live in style. It was she who through Alexey, supported him, financially if not emotionally; he liked gambling and he liked his drink.

Of course you know all this! But when one is writing a novel one doesn't always get the proportions right – the emphasis, I mean. It's like playing the piano, the pianist interprets a piece one way, and the listener another, and they each think they know what the composer meant!

By the way, you didn't say what you thought about the *finale*, and whether it satisfied the challenge of Nature and of Art. But now I remember, you hadn't got as far as that.

To turn to a more agreeable subject – yourself, your dear self. Art can be an escape from life, or a substitute for life, or an enhancement of life. I think most artists have found it an enhancement. All the same, it isn't the same thing as life. The painter paints what he sees, the sculptor sculpts what he sees, or used to; but the architect, the composer, the poet and the novelist have to dig what they can out of their own entrails, and when that source of supply is exhausted, they have to wait for another, or else dry up – a fate which has befallen many an artist besides Rimbaud. Experience often comes to their help, but not always – for sometimes it is worn out, burnt out, and sometimes it is repetitive, a faint mocking echo of a voice which once thrilled and inspired them, but no longer.

Whereas with human relationships, friendships, *love*, such

drying up of the well-springs needn't occur, for Nature, with most people, at any rate, is reciprocal, and demands that one voice should be answered by another – not the voice of art, the *alter ego* of the artist, with whom he is always in conference, whether he likes it or not. Nor does he always get a reply: the *alter ego* sulks and skulks, and won't play, won't vouchsafe an answer!

Alexey wasn't an artist of any sort: he was, as you know, a man who had done well enough in business to be able to retire in his late forties. I could never decide what business it was (marmalade? steel?) for I know so little about business, but he was good at it, and after his retirement still held two or three directorships, so he was quite comfortably off.

I didn't say at what point in his career he met Pauline, but I think it was before his retirement. She wasn't his *alter ego*, but she supplied him with something that office-hours and board-meetings didn't. He was romantic at heart, as so many business men are, I'm told, and she embodied, she was the object, of his romantic feelings, which he inflicted on her quite relentlessly. She tried to be kind to him (as she had reason to be), and she did her best for him, but *her* romantic feelings were centred on this motor-mechanic, he who was in and out of garages. The money she gave him was either what she had earned herself and could spare out of her exacting budget, or the money that Alexey gave her. Alexey would have given her much more, but she was scrupulous and rather proud, and since she wasn't to him what he would have liked her to be, she didn't want to accept from him more than she thought was a fair reward for all the time and trouble, and money, he had spent on her.

He entertained her at fashionable restaurants where she enjoyed the expensive food, and was as glad to be seen with him as he was glad to be seen with her – for having appeared on television as well as on the stage, and occasionally in films, she was a celebrity in a small way. When she came into a restaurant, people looked up and sometimes nudged each other; and he, little as he wanted to share her with the general public, or with anyone else, couldn't help being pleased by the admiring glances cast in their direction.

He knew about Jock, of course; he had found them together when once or twice he had visited her unexpectedly in her flat. Usually he was punctilious about giving her notice beforehand, but sometimes, I suppose, his loneliness got the better of him.

It must have been an embarrassing encounter, with Jock oily and greasy and dirty in his working-clothes, and perhaps unshaven, but Pauline liked him better that way than when he had smartened himself up and looked neither fish nor flesh, though more flesh than fish, for his fleshy aspect stood out a mile, especially when he took his jacket off to make himself comfortable, and rolled his shirt-sleeves up over his muscular, hairy forearms. When Pauline first introduced them to each other Alexey took Jock to be an electrician or a plumber or some engineer whom Pauline had called in, for the mechanical arrangements of the flat were always needing attention. The two men stared, rather than glared at each other, for although Jock knew something about Alexey, Alexey had never heard of Jock. But on the level of a mutual lack of understanding they both behaved very well, each with the manners he had been brought up to, which, though very different, demanded (if no quarrel was afoot) politeness in the presence of a lady.

Afterwards Pauline explained to Alexey that Jock was an old friend of hers and part of her varied social background. This Alexey accepted for he was still too much infatuated with her to resent, or even to criticize, anything she said or did. Jock had his place in her life and he had his; it did not occur to Alexey, then, to wonder which was uppermost.

All this, dear Elizabeth, comes into a later part of the story. You may have read it by now, but it won't convey quite the same impression; I have often found that if I try to tell the 'plot' of a novel to a friend it turns out to be different from the one I have fashioned for myself or for the public!

But I do apologize – I meant to write to you, and about you, and *not* about the baseless fabric of my vision. *You* are *partly* to blame – you showed so much interest in those early chapters, and like a proud mother, I couldn't help expatiating on the qualities of my latest child.

But I do feel so concerned for you and the breach – for it must amount to a breach – with Frank. Even if you asked my advice (actually, looking back at your letter, I see you did!) I shouldn't know how to advise you.

> I'll not offer you advice
> Till you please to ask me thrice,
> Which if you in scorn reject
> T'will be just as I expect.

It is clear (to me) that you are fed up with Frank and equally clear that you have every right to be. *Que faire?* One's life is of oneself a thing apart; it is like a house that one has bought, or built, or inherited: one lives in it, but it has an existence of its own, outside oneself; an existence that one has helped to create, just as one may have helped to create a child. Afterwards, like a child, it goes its own way, but like a child, we are still bound to it, and it to us, unless we discard it, and get another house, or get, or beget, another child.

What I'm trying to say is that one's past life, and one's present life, for that matter, are built up out of the accumulations of the past, the accumulations of experience which one cannot shed, however much one would like to, any more than the pilgrim in *Pilgrim's Progress* could shed his burden. The burden is part of oneself.

At the same time I feel most strongly that one cannot, and must not, go on living with someone whom one dislikes. Unfaithfulness isn't, in my view, a sufficient cause for parting; we are all of us, married or not, unfaithful to each other in thought, word or deed. Unfaithfulness, in one or the other partner (I speak from observation only) can co-exist with *liking*, and even with loving. But liking is more important; and if unfaithfulness destroys *liking*, the time has come to part. It is unbearable to live in the same house, in the same room, in the same bed, with someone you really dislike.

I gather you dislike Frank because of his infidelities – which is reason enough though a negative one – not because you like someone else better, which would be a positive one (a plus gesture is preferable to a minus!) If you want to leave him for someone else, I should; if not, I shouldn't, remembering the life you have made for yourself in Canada, the many friends, and the familiarity of the set-up.

And then the change to London, where no doubt you have many friends, and will make more. You won't have to make a friend of *me*, such as I am – but London isn't what it was, and I, if our circumstances were reversed, should think twice about emigrating to Canada. Kind as the people are there, I should miss the *familiarity*, and the myriad little things that compose it. I should feel *hors de mon assiette* (as no doubt they would say in Quebec). Familiarity is the bread of life, just as routine is. They have few to sing their praises, but they are essential to happiness, at least they are to mine.

I love the little two-storey houses in the winding wandering streets (their names written up in ample rotund eighteenth-century lettering) round the block of converted flats in which I live. I love my flat, not so much for itself, and it isn't just one more cell in the universal bee-hive, but because it is *familiar*, and so is my henchman Paolo, in more ways than one! And so is my bed. People often say, 'I don't sleep well in a strange bed' (it is one of the few tributes to the power of familiarity), and I respectfully agree with them, although no doubt there is something to be said for a strange bed-fellow! I should hate to be *uprooted*, and find myself in unfamiliar surroundings, where I should have to discover new tradesmen, who wouldn't allow me credit, new friends who might not give me much credit (if you see what I mean) either, and a whole new range of thoughts and feelings and impressions, so that I should hardly be able to recognize myself!

Individualist though I am, I depend for half my happiness on my context, and the feeling of security which this little corner of South Kensington gives me. And my fear is lest, if you abandoned your no doubt much wider context in Quebec for a London context, you would feel like a fish out of water. For one thing, London is completely changed from the London you knew twenty years ago. Even the streets go different ways, at least the traffic does, and you would find many other kinds of frustration that I'm sure don't impede your path in Canada, land of the free! – at least that's how I think of it. 'Gentlemen, I would rather have written those lines than take Quebec!' General Wolfe is supposed to have said, but I doubt if he would say so now, here in England when he would be liable to be bowler-hatted in some cottage near Stoke Poges instead of scaling the Heights of Abraham.

Don't for a moment imagine that I am trying to dissuade you from coming back: I, for one, should welcome you with open arms and do my best to make the narrow confines of Onslow Gate resemble the broad boulevards of Quebec. It would enlarge my context, which I know is shrinking: but mightn't it constrict yours? To me, the solution to your situation, your predicament, your quandary – as Henry James might have put it – rests entirely on the personal question: Do you dislike Frank too much to go on living with him? Is there someone else? I feel there may be, and if there is, I think that Quebec, with its forward-looking viewpoint, would be more like home to you than London, with its hold-ups and stoppages and traffic-blocks, both physical and metaphorical.

There is just one thing more I want to say, dear Elizabeth, and I have been debating with myself whether I should say it, and I hesitate all the more because of the kind things *you* said about *The Love-Adept* (and you may not like it as well when you have finished it!), and because it sounds so ungrateful. But I hate to sail under false colours and we never have, have we? Truth is the first priority in normal life (if there is such a thing) as in war it is the first casualty. How I ramble on, trying not to say what I know I ought to say!

Never mind, out with it! All my books are, in a sense dedicated to you, but *The Love-Adept* was in fact dedicated to another Elizabeth. I know that this won't make any difference to your opinion of the book or your opinion of me – still less your opinion of yourself! But if someone says 'How can James G. (I sometimes forget that my surname is Golightly, it is so unsuitable to my heavy plodding progress), 'How *can* James G. have dedicated that *awful* book to you? Why did you let him?' You can either reply, 'I didn't let him, he did it without my permission', or you can say, 'Oh, it was another Elizabeth. I don't know who she is, and I don't care. She may not exist, Elizabeth is a common name, it hardly means more than "woman". Whoever she may be, good luck to her.'

And good luck to you, dearest Elizabeth, either in Canada or here.

> With much love,
> James

CHAPTER III

48 *Clarence Terrace,*
Regent's Park, N.W.1.

Dearest James,

I have just received the latest effusion of your pen, and I can never tell you how overwhelmed I am, how *bowled over*, to use a cricketing term (if it is a cricketing term – 'bowled' and 'over' certainly are) but cricket is such a mild game to express the feelings I had when I read my name on the title page. To have had a book dedicated to me, and by you! It is really *too* much. But 'is it cricket?' Is it 'playing the game?' I mean, shouldn't someone else have had the honour of the *dédicace*? I know so little about games and gamesmanship. You must enlighten me.

Don't imagine I am looking your gift-horse in the mouth, far from it, but having been brought up to regard humility as a virtue, I wonder if I shan't become *swollen with pride*, which would be a pity, as I am overweight anyhow!

But apart from the honour of the *dédicace*, I am fascinated by the book itself, and I wonder what gave you the idea for it! I can't help seeing certain likenesses between you and Alexey, but I've never thought of you as a love-adept. I know the quotation, but I can't think of you as 'sleeping on a poet's lips', which would anyhow be unsuitable to one of your sex – although I suppose a poet *could* be a *poetess*, a word that some women poets, e.g. Edith Sitwell, very much resent as being derogatory, although I don't see why they should. A prophetess

23

is not less than a prophet, or a sorceress less than a sorcerer. It only marks a distinction of *sex*, rather desirable nowadays, like a label on one's luggage, when the sexes are so mixed up.

I try to tease you, don't I? But I am sure that others besides me will see a likeness between you and Alexey. It is nothing to be ashamed of, for he was a nice man, more sinned against than sinning, if one can mention 'sin' in this day and age; and you yourself have told me that you couldn't altogether keep yourself out of your novels. You have ploughed with your own heifer – to use, or misuse, a Biblical – agricultural phrase.

But what rather upsets my diagnosis is that I can't reconcile you, the James I have known and *revered* (I mustn't put it more strongly) for so many years, with the love-adept, Alexey. I have always thought of you as a light-o'-love, flitting from flower to flower, of which I may once have been one – the lesser celandine, perhaps – in your career of amatory botanizing, I *can't* see you as a kind of masculine Patient Grizel, such as Alexey was, pursuing his mistress (if she *was* his mistress – you don't make that quite clear) from one provincial town to another, always turning up at the end of a performance with a bunch of flowers when she was tired out, and longing for bed, and perhaps for the embraces of Jock, who was then acting as her chauffeur-extraordinary.

I very much enjoyed your description of Pauline's first meeting with Alexey, after he had been so carried away by her performance in *The Scythian Queen* that he sent up his card and was admitted to her dressing-room (or her green-room, as you called it in your old-fashioned way). He expected a rebuff – he was astonished to be let in – and more astonished when he found her in floods of tears, for the Scythian Queen had been through a great deal including the ordeal of watching her lover beheaded. Most actresses, he thought, remained unmoved by the emotional aspect of their parts – they *have* to, just as doctors have to be unmoved, or comparatively unmoved, by the sufferings of their patients. Otherwise they simply couldn't carry on, the double strain would be too great. When he presented her with his bouquet (looking, as you said, everywhere but at her, so great was his embarrassment and his feeling of intrusion on her simulated grief) she burst into tears afresh, and he was going to back out, without a word, when she begged him to stay, saying 'You have made everything different for me'.

And I enjoyed too, so much, your account of her meeting, not long before, with Jock at the garage. She was on her way to some outlandish but (for her) important place, Halifax, I think, and unlike most actors and actresses on tour (did you check up on this James?) she didn't travel by train but drove her own car, and then on some lonely Yorkshire moor her car broke down. I don't feel sure that she would have found a garage there, but thank goodness she did, and there was Jock, in his overalls, ready to help. Jock with his black hair coming to a peak on his forehead, his deep blue eyes (a Scottish Highland type, I suppose) and his Adonis-cum-Hercules appearance.

He fixed the car for her in a trice, not so quickly as she fell for him but more quickly than, afterwards, he fell for her. Thanks to him she was able to keep her engagement at Halifax, or wherever it was; thanks to her, he was able to buy an interest in the garage, though his responsibilities to her did not end there – not by any means.

All this, of course, you must know so well, that it is idiotic of me to repeat it to you. My chief excuse is that these scenes keep running in my head like a recurring tune, and that by playing them back, so to speak, to you I can clear my mind of things that compete obsessively for my attention, such as the idea of Alexey, or you! – running after a woman, and spending uncomfortable nights in provincial hotels, armed with a bouquet of unseasonable roses! Somehow it seems too *droll*, and no doubt that is one reason why I keep thinking of it. You once told me I was ruled by my subconscious mind, and another time you told me I was ruled by my sense of humour, which shows you aren't really a good psychologist, for the two allegiances are incompatible – the subconscious self has no sense of humour, it is there just as a *warning*, like the red light on a traffic-signal, and woe betide you if you disregard it!

Alexey must have obeyed it only too well when he started on that will-o'-the wisp chase after his darling Pauline, in the Austin Princess, provided by Alexey but driven by her boy-friend Jock – her E-type Jaguar having been discarded as too antique. She ought to have given him (Alexey) a severe snub, as I would have, and told him to remember his age (46, I think you said), and not to be so silly. But I suppose we are all silly at one time or another, and especially at *that* age (I am nearing it myself).

Jock was the least silly: he got what he wanted from Pauline, in the way of money and sex, and no doubt a sort of romantic réclame (if he valued such a thing) from being the *cavaliere servente* of a fairly well-known actress. And she got what she wanted – his companionship by day and by night – the latter was more important to her, for she wasn't particular, (or *was* she particular?) in such matters. The stage has, and always has had, rules of its own where the emotional life is concerned.

And Alexey, what did he get out of it? Only the satisfaction of following her around, adoring her from afar, and sometimes from near, and helping to keep her and Jock in funds, and Jock's two children in comparative comfort. You make it clear that he didn't *resent* Jock, nor did Jock resent him (no doubt he couldn't, knowing or suspecting that though Pauline always paid his wages, most of the money came from Alexey), and in fact they were on quite good terms, when Pauline in her furs got into the front seat beside the driver, and Alexey took the back seat.

Such a different world from mine, and my work with the National Trust, which doesn't include romantic encounters in theatres or garages, or the *bonhomie* of sugar-daddies, such as Alexey was.

But what happened to the trio in the end? This is what I long to know, and can't find out, because a friend of mine came in and saw me reading your book, and at once asked if she could borrow it. I said, No, she must either buy it herself or get it from a library. But she would take no refusal; she said she would return it to me the next day without fail. But three days have passed, and she hasn't returned it – either because she has been reading or re-reading it or because – well my imagination boggles. She can't have *lost* it, can she, James? Or put it down somewhere and forgotten about it? Who could treat a book of yours in such a disregardful fashion? I implored her to send it back to me, and it maddens me to think that she knows what happened to Pauline and Alexey and Jock, and I don't! But people are so unscrupulous about books – they are more precious than rubies, as I told her more than once, and showed her the page, where you had dedicated it to *me*! I am sure no one has ever dedicated a book to *her*, but she must know what it means, even if she has never had an Alexey trailing after her!

I *think* I know what happened in the end, but I'm not *sure*, so do be an angel, dear James, and tell me, in case Caroline doesn't return the book. I shall get it out of her in the end, of course, even if I have to *threaten* her. Perhaps you will think I ought to get another copy from the library, but I should have to wait a long time for that – or else I ought to *buy* one, but books are so expensive, even yours is, and I have no Alexey to foot my bills! Besides, yours is a very special copy and I feel I am nearer to you when I am reading it. So I shall expect to hear from you.

Meanwhile, all my love, and all my thanks for the book and all the pleasure it has given and will give me.

Yours,
Elizabeth

CHAPTER IV

117 Chillinghurst Court,
S.W.7.

Dearest Elizabeth,

Thank you so much for your letter and do forgive me for not answering it sooner, but I have been away and I only got it – along with another letter which I didn't enjoy half so much, in fact not at all – when I got back this morning.

The Love-Adept hasn't come out yet – yours was one of the advance copies my kind publishers send me. It will be out on Monday week I think, if they are as good as their word. And then you may, or may not see, how the story ends. Some reviewers are quite unscrupulous about 'giving away' the dénouement of a novel, which *I* think takes away half the pleasure of reading it, because it pricks the bubble of suspense which one has been (at least I have been) at such pains to blow up.

I know that the best novelists don't rely on suspense; their novels *develop*, and the reader follows the development to its perhaps inevitable end. One doesn't know exactly, for instance, how *Madame Bovary* will end, but one knows that it will end unhappily, for Emma was a self-destroying character who could only come to a bad end, just as one knows for a different reason that Jane Austen's novels will have a happy ending. With her temperament, and her conception of the novel as essentially an 'entertainment' (you couldn't call *Madame Bovary* an 'entertainment', without stretching the meaning of the word, unless you were completely heartless), you know what to expect.

All the same, neither Jane Austen nor a good many other great novelists were above springing a surprise or two on the reader, if only in matters of detail; and some went further than detail. Who could foretell, for instance, the ending of *Les Liaisons Dangereuses* and the way in which Laclos, who has all along shown the forces of Evil as successful and indeed paramount, always having things their own way, and intelligent and *amusing*, compared to the miserably equipped forces of the Good, suddenly, and convincingly turns the tables on M. de Valmont and Madame de Merteuil? It is one of the greatest surprises and to me one of the greatest shocks in fiction.

And even Cervantes, the wisest and the most humane of novelists, keeps a number of tricks up his sleeve, and most of all in the ending which he hurries over in a casual fashion, with no effect of *empressment* or built-up climax, but which does, in an extraordinary way, in a few pages, sum up and fulfil the meaning and intention of the whole book.

Forgive this long preamble, but it was meant to excuse and even to defend the element of surprise which seems to me an essential element in the art of fiction. No doubt inevitability should be the prime mover, but I have never been able to achieve it.

However, what I meant to say was, don't feel annoyed with me, please, dear Elizabeth, if I don't tell you what happens at the end of *The Love-Adept*. You will think I am making a fuss about nothing – you always think I make a fuss about nothing, and often tease me about it. I love being teased by you, though not by everyone. I should hate to tease you in return, even if I knew how to. I'm not doing that, I don't want to seem captious and silly, but you know how I dislike discussing my 'work' before it is published, feeling the same that one does when one gives someone a present: it isn't half the fun, for them or for you, if you tell them what the present is going to be, and they may get wrong ideas about it, founded on their hopes or wishes, and be bitterly disappointed when it comes!

Of course these parental misgivings shouldn't apply to *The Love-Adept* which is, for good or ill, a *fait accompli*: I cannot cancel half a line, nor all my tears wash out a word of it! All the same I have a superstitious feeling that I would rather you read the rest of the book yourself (I don't quite remember where you had got to) than in the light of my interpretations, which may be mistaken and anyhow quite different from yours. I should like to know what you think before I tell you what I think. A fresh eye sees better than an old I (I don't apologise for the pun, since Shakespeare made it), and if you don't see eye to eye with me as to how the story should have ended, well, that is just too bad. Disagreement is often more salutary though not so gratifying as agreement. You were never a yes-woman (no offence intended), and I would much rather hear your own opinion than your opinion diluted with mine.

So I hope your thievish friend (I think I can guess who she is) will buck up and send the book back, and if she says she can't tie up a parcel, you must give her a piece of your mind – she can well afford a gift of that sort. The moral is, neither a borrower nor a lender be. If she says she has lost it, I will get my bookseller to send you another copy and charge it up to her (if she is who I think she is).

But there *is* something I should like to say about the book, in spite of my disinclination to say anything, and it has a bearing on the ending – because I don't think I made enough of it. Jock didn't miss a trick of course – he was a Ulysses type, and would have thought himself a mug if he hadn't extracted every bawbee out of his situation, his two situations, vis-à-vis Pauline and Alexey. Alexey, you may remember – if you got as far as that – had been trailing Pauline for some time before her Isolde-like meeting with Jock at the Yorkshire garage. And she might never have met him, and certainly would not have *affiché'd* herself to him, if Alexey had been with her at the time. But Alexey couldn't drive; after he met Pauline he realized what an asset it would be to him in his relationship with Pauline, who was always on the wing (when not in the wings) if he knew how to. But try as he would, he couldn't pass his driving-test. At every critical juncture he was always thinking of something else – Pauline probably – and didn't do the right thing. I thought of him as an obsessive character with one end in view. His single-mindedness had been a help to him in board-rooms, where he knew what to aim at and what to ignore, but it didn't help him to adjust himself to motor traffic which was always presenting him with new problems and no time to solve them in.

So after repeated failures which reduced him in his own regard, and in Pauline's regard for him, he gave up the unequal struggle. This didn't mean that he didn't often accompany Pauline in her tours of the provinces but he was a passenger, it was she who took the wheel, and this gave him a feeling of inferiority, as many other of her qualities did.

Thus it happened that she was alone when her car limped into the Carnaby Moor garage on a dark evening in winter and Jock fixed it for her, and fixed himself in her affections, for she was an impulsive as well as a beautiful woman, and it would never have occurred to her to resist what might be only a passing whim. She was then in funds, her funds and Alexey's, and she used them and her looks, to persuade the garage-proprietor to let Jock drive her to her destination, in case she should have another breakdown on the way. He asked for time to smarten himself up, and re-appeared in an incredibly short space of time, looking more like a gentleman than a gentleman ought to look. To Pauline he had lost some of his glamour, but he was much more acceptable to the hotel than he would have been in his overalls.

Next day, at crack of dawn, he returned by train to Carnaby Moor, with a letter in his pocket saying that Mrs. Pauline Merryweather had engaged him to be her chauffeur and handyman (I myself was never quite clear why she wanted a handyman, since she lived in a flat with 'porterage'), at a salary of £25 a week, all found.

The salary was more than Jock had been receiving at the garage; and the 'all found' made a lot of difference: it would enable him to keep the two children his ex-wife had left him to provide for. She had taken herself off one night, leaving him, the little girl, Jean, aged ten, and the little boy, Fergus, aged seven. He woke up one morning to find them there, in their littls cots, but not her, nor had he been able to trace her. They needed dressing, and they needed washing, they needed feeding, they needed all sorts of things: their existence, for him, was summed up in the word 'needs'. He didn't shirk these needs, but being a needy man himself, he couldn't meet them. He found a kind-hearted woman to look after them. He paid her as little as he could, but what little he paid left him nearly destitute.

He was fond of them and liked to hear them call him 'Dad', on the infrequent occasions when his work at the garage allowed him to see them.

His 'engagement' with Pauline would end this financial stringency, temporarily. He knew the effect his good looks had on women; he also knew how short-lived it was, and how short-lived it had been in the case of his wife. He wasn't cruel; he drank too much perhaps, but what Scotsman of his class and occupation didn't? He wasn't under the illusion that his job with Mrs. Merryweather would last long, but it was worth trying, and meanwhile it would be nice to see the world, or as much of it (England mostly) as she covered in her theatrical activities. He was shrewd enough to know that if Pauline's *faible* for him died out, he would be left on the rocks.

When he accepted her offer, Alexey was in London. But it wasn't long before he appeared on the scene, shortish and middle-aged compared with Jock, and very well dressed. Now where do I stand? Jock asked himself.

His first conclusion was that Alexey would resent him trying to oust him: at sight of each other they would bristle, like two hostile dogs. And that was his reaction when Alexey first appeared and sat in the back seat, leaving him and Pauline in front.

Who is this bloke, he asked himself – for Pauline, who never explained anything, hadn't told him about Alexey. It'll be either him or me. And for once he made a mistake in changing gear.

He must dislike me, Jock thought. He *must* dislike me, it wouldn't be human if he didn't, being such a close friend of Miss Pauline as he seems to be, unless he doesn't know, or guess, what our relations are? She kept turning round and talking to him, and once she said 'This is Jock, he's my chauffeur. I forgot to introduce you to each other' (although she had). He bent forward and Jock tried to look round; only just escaping an accident. Women, Jock warned himself, think you can drive on the tip of their tongues, so to speak. 'I'm glad to meet you, Jock,' Alexey said, 'and I hope we shall have many drives together. Mrs. Merryweather needs someone to drive her, and I can't, worse luck.'

'But you do drive me, Alexey,' she said, 'not in the car of course, I wouldn't trust myself to you, even if you had passed your driving-test, but in other ways you are a perfect slave-driver!'

Mr. Alexey (Jock didn't know then what his other name was, it was something Russian or Polish or Czech, that no one could ever pronounce, that was why he called himself Mr. Alexey) – anyhow he didn't answer, but he said a moment later,

'Shall we dine at the Berkeley?'

'When did we dine there last?' Miss Pauline asked.

'Oh, about a week ago.'

'Well, let's go there,' she said, 'it's as good as anywhere.'

Jock detected the note of boredom in her voice (he could always tell if a woman was bored or interested), and was surprised, for he would have been arse-over-tip with joy if someone had asked him to dine at the Berkeley. He had, actually, dined alone with Miss Pauline at several places, theatrical joints they were, where anyone can meet anyone, and no questions asked, but nowhere as grand as the Berkeley. And he was still more surprised when he heard Alexey say,

'What about Jock?'

'Oh, Jock,' she said vaguely, as if he was someone she hardly knew. 'Oh, Jock likes to dine by himself, don't you, Jock? Get yourself a good dinner, and call for us about 10.30.'

'Very good, Madam,' Jock said.

He supposed she thought Mr. Alexey wouldn't like it if she asked him to dine with them, but they must have talked it over, because later on Miss Pauline often asked Jock to join them at meals. He used to feel rather awkward at first, especially as he came from Glasgow, and English people couldn't always understand what he said, but he soon got used to it, and drink always helps. He had never drunk wine before, or only a glass of Red Biddy now and then, which of course they didn't touch. But he soon got used to vin rouge and vin blanc, and quite enjoyed it.

Jock never kidded himself that this would last, but he said to himself, 'Jock, while the going is good' – and who could

B*

blame him, least of all Fergus and Jean, who had better clothes, and better food, and better treatment from old Mrs. Kirkwood than they used to have, when he had to scrape and save, and deny himself a drop of Scotch so that they could have a new outfit. Children grow so fast, you wouldn't believe it.

But all the time Jock had his eye on Mr. Alexey, as he came to call him, and couldn't understand why he put up with this triangular relationship (an English working-man might not know what this means, but the Scots are better educated – thank God).

Jock thought that Mr. Alexey must know that he went to bed with Miss Pauline, just as Jock knew from the way they talked, and the way she looked at him, and in ever so many other ways, that Mr. Alexey didn't have sex with her. So why was he following her around to all sorts of outlandish places, and giving her expensive meals, and money, yes, *money* – without which, he soon realised, she couldn't have afforded to pay him his wages and his room at Mrs. Kirkwood's which he shared with the kids? What was *he* getting out of it? Jock asked himself. Nothing but her company as far as he could see, and the sort of status-feeling any man gets being seen with a good-looking woman.

It beats me, thought Jock. Whoever pays the piper calls the tune. Mr. Alexey was a soft-mannered man, who wouldn't have hurt a fly, but every day he expected to hear him say, 'Jock, I'm sorry to have to tell you this, but Mrs. Merry-weather doesn't need your services any longer.' If they ever had to take a tough line with anyone – (and the theatrical world is no joke, believe me – they don't spare each other's feelings), she always left it to Jock. 'She's had rather a thin time, just lately, money-wise, so she must ask you to take a week's notice,' and he should reply, 'Yes sir', or 'Yes, Mr. Alexey, please thank Madam very much for all her kindness which will be remembered with gratitude, and yours too, sir'. Such bull-shit – but one has one's self-respect.

And every day that Jock saw Mr. Alexey growing more and more love-sick (I can use no other term) and more and more disappointed with what Pauline wouldn't and couldn't, give him (sex or affection or no matter what), Jock had his answer ready. He felt sorry for him, he honestly did, for he behaved like a gentleman, to her and to him, and Jock didn't like to see him suffer, and perhaps, if it hadn't been for the bairns, he would have asked for his cards and left him to get on with it. But he didn't, of course, and when it finally happened, it happened in a different way from what Jock expected. He was surprised, and there aren't many things that can surprise a Scotsman, especially a Campbell from Fifeshire.

I have scribbled out Jock's interior monologue, dear Elizabeth, because although the substance of it is in the book (if you have got so far) I may have represented Jock as more of a gold-digger than he really was, and when a character has lodged in one's imagination for a long time, even if not in search of an author, so to speak, one feels a certain responsibility towards him (or her) and doesn't want to do them an injustice. So please feel as kindly as you can towards Pauline and Jock – Alexey, apart from the fact that he was a fool, is too obviously an object of pity.

I hope you won't be cross with me or think me childish for not wanting to tell you exactly how the story ends. It spoils my interest in a novel, or takes some of it away – if I know beforehand what the end is going to be – it is as though the traditional carrot was to stop dangling before the donkey's mouth. (Forgive me, the metaphor doesn't fit you, you are realistic, you can eat your carrot and have it, but it does apply to me, who needs the constant stimulus of something I can't reach. A minor twentieth-century Tantalus, I suppose, but I'm not the only one!)

There *is* one more thing I want to say, which has nothing to do with *The Love-Adept*, as a novel, but which has something to do with your kind appreciation of it. I don't know how to say it, it sounds so ungrateful and so ungracious, and almost as if I had told you a lie, which, dear Elizabeth, I would never do. Not that you would mind very much if you caught me out – you would just tease me about it afterwards. Well – a deep breath – it is this. Why do so many women have the same Christian name? They ought to have a number attached to it, as some American families do after their surnames, not to emphasize their identity, but to show where they come in the family tree. Well, I have made a short story long, but what I wanted to say was – and it may amuse you – the Elizabeth I dedicated *The Love-Adept* to wasn't, on *paper*, on the printed page, you, it was another Elizabeth of the same name. What more can I say (to quote the writer of the Epistle to the Hebrews, of whom you are not one!) than that it brought you my love, just as your most understanding letter deserves, to put it mildly, my most grateful thanks.

Yours,
James

CHAPTER V

191, Adelaide Terrace,
S.W.3.

Dear James,

Thank you very much for letting me have a pre-view of your novel, *The Love-Adept*, and thank you still more for dedicating it to me. No one has ever dedicated a book to me before, although I have been a fiction-reviewer for many years. Perhaps that's why.

I hope I have always kept my integrity as a critic, and it's only fair to tell you that I don't like this last book of yours at all, and I am rather surprised that you dedicated it to me. If it is sent to me to review, I shall have to say that I don't like it, which will be disagreeable, but after all, no one can know that 'Elizabeth' is meant for me, unless I tell them, which I certainly shan't. I *could* say it was dedicated to the memory of Elizabeth – *Elizabeth and her German Garden*, who is long since dead, much longer than your book has been or soon will be. It is to come out on Monday week your publishers' announcement says.

I quite liked some of your novels in the old days, and I said so, both to you and in the Press, which is perhaps why you made this rather belated gesture to me. At that time, how many years ago, you were contemporary or nearly. But as the world has been growing younger, you have been growing older, and you are now sadly behind the times. Forgive me for saying this.

Now, first as regards the novel itself, its subject-matter, its theme, its characters, its general what-have-you.

I find the central situation dated, banal, and unoriginal to the point of being plagiaristic. The glamorous actress, the faithful swain who dogs her footsteps, and the handsome chauffeur who comes between them – 'are not all these things written' (as the Bible says) written, *mutatis mutandis*, once and for all in *Lady Chatterley's Lover*, which is not one of my favourite books but which is obviously one of yours, for you used the same situation, I seem to remember, in an earlier novel. This situation seems to haunt your mind, goodness knows why, like a recurring tune.

With which of the trio do you identify yourself, I wonder? With Pauline, beautiful, vigorous, energetic, bored – I don't think many actresses are bored? Or with Alexey, also bored, but longing to be taken out of himself by inflicting his boredom on Pauline who tries to tolerate it for the sake of the money he gives her? Or do you see yourself in the role of Jock, who would be bored if he had time to be, and in any case is himself boring, unless you find an anatomical figure, stripped of its clothes, intrinsically interesting?

Perhaps you see yourself as all three, perhaps as none of them. I hope the latter, for you don't get under any of their skins, and skin is the only reality they have to offer, for all your efforts to individualize them.

I admit that there are still a good many people even today who have enough money to subsidize actresses and their attendant boy-friends. And I must say you don't pretend to be shocked by their behaviour, as you would have been at one time, how well I remember it! You even pretended to be shocked by *me*. You must have got over that by now, or you wouldn't have dedicated your book to me.

It may sound inconsistent when I say that as a work of art

The Love-Adept would have gained if it had shocked you. *Oeuf sur le plat* tempts the appetite of many readers, and is an easy dish for some novelists to prepare, but it isn't right for you. All the time I was reading the book I could hear you saying to yourself, congratulating yourself, 'How tolerant I am! Dear Reader, please note that I don't condemn any of these people. I let them go their own way, as they would have in life; I am not censorious about them. I realise that most people nowadays are totally materialistic in their outlook, unless their materialism is dominated by sex'. Pauline, I should say, was dominated by both; Jock by material considerations; and Alexey – well, I don't know. He doesn't seem to me a credible figure, but no doubt a psychoanalyst could explain him.

You bend over backwards, as they say, in order to seem a man of your day – not of your *age* – dear James! But in my view it's a dismal failure. You don't realize that people of today don't want to step out of the ruck: they want to be in it and *with* it, in all senses of the term. They want to keep up with the Joneses, they don't want to outstrip them, they just want to be *with* them, they are ruled by *fashion*, a factor you never seem to take into account, but fashion is the ruling passion, and of course it doesn't encourage individualism, or eccentricity, how could it? If you had a million Paulines, a million Alexeys and a million Jocks all behaving in the same way, to make a pattern of behaviour that would be acceptable to the teenagers, then you might be getting somewhere. But they only want the emotions that are within their range and by which they can be communicably excited, such as train-wrecking, telephone-kiosk breaking, throwing bottles at football matches, fighting with each other at the sea-side, here or abroad, or battling with the police and then accusing them of brutality. Apart from these stimulants, this release for their egos, their ideal, which they will never realize, is to bask semi-nude on a deck-chair or some ocean-going cruise, or to bask, still semi-nude, on the beach of some West-Indian island, ready for a bathe or just returned from a bathe, with the sub-tropical sun beating down on their nicely tanned or badly blistered bodies, and a white-coated black-faced waiter hovering by, handing out dry martinis.

I don't say that I approve of this as a solution of our present discontents, but I do say that by ignoring it, you vitiate the value of your novel as a social document, which every novel must be.

Imagining themselves gazing, mindless, into the cloudless blue of the Bahamas, Pauline and Alexey and even Jock would forget their personal problems, and who owed money to whom, and who hoped for money from whom, who gave themselves to whom – or just who gave themselves up to the joys of millions of others, like themselves, intent on holiday-making beneath southern skies.

You may laugh, James, you may laugh, although I don't find much humour in your book, at least not the kind that most readers today would think funny. Funny peculiar, perhaps, but not funny ha-ha! Humour draws people together of course; if you told a funny story at a party or a pub, and the listeners drew away from you instead of drawing nearer to you, you would know it had been a flop. But they would only draw nearer to you if it was a kind of 'sick' humour, a joke about the atom-bomb, perhaps, something which draws people together because of the common evil threatening us. No, evil is a question-begging word; the common calamity that is likely to overtake us. Your humour isn't always meant to be kind; but it is meant to suggest that the rather ridiculous (not funny) manœuvres of Pauline and Alexey and Jock are *exceptional*, enacted against a general background of happiness and reasonableness, and to get any effect they do get from the contrast. Whereas there is no happiness or reasonableness today, or if there is, I don't see it. What I – what we – for I think the word and the conception of 'I' is becoming redundant if not obsolete – are confronted with is a common recognition of the evil – no, not the evil – the extreme unpleasantness of what lies ahead of us, and we find such humour as we can, in brief (remember, in brief) comments on that unpleasantness. Our contemporaries are in tune with it, they are 'with it'; they are not in contrast with it, they are intensifications of it.

The old joke of somebody slipping up on a piece of orange-peel got its point from the fact that he or she was an exception: they were to be laughed at because other people *didn't* slip on orange-peel. We could congratulate ourselves that we were cleverer and more fortunate than they and burst into peals of laughter (no pun intended). But we can't now, because there is orange-peel under everybody's foot.

So your effort to make your trio seem different, and perhaps superior, to the rest of us on the ground of their exceptional circumstances, didn't cut any ice with me. Indeed, they were luckier than most people, because they had Alexey's money to fall back on. I could see perfectly well what you were working up to, Pauline and Jock, secure in their sexual bond, move off together, having acquired a good dollop of Alexey's money, leaving him in misery and comparative poverty, to commit suicide. He had put all his eggs, or should I say his ego, into one, or perhaps I should say two baskets, and there was no other way out for him. You will shed tears over him and expect the reader to. I couldn't, and frankly I couldn't finish the book. Not that it exactly bored me but because it is so out of date. If you had read any science fiction, or recent French novels, you would realize that the future, if there is one, is in the hands of people, not of persons.

The chapter where the two children are talking to each other, is an example of what I mean. They talk like little grown-ups, each aware of the other's identity, and playing up or playing down to it as adults do, not as children would, recognizing their childhood as their own special province, in which grown-ups are seen distantly and dimly as trees walking. At least it used to be so. Nowadays they probably regard their elders (but not their betters, oh no, James) as enemies or potential enemies, who would probably frown on, or still worse ignore, their proper pastimes of train-wrecking, bottle-throwing, and so on.

When I say 'proper', I use the word in its original, its 'proper' sense, meaning the pastimes that are natural, inevitable and as some would say, desirable in human units of their age, in both senses of the word, under-privileged units deprived of the dubious advantages of parental care. They see parental care, in so far as they enjoy or suffer from it, as something restricting, or frustrating, the pleasure-patterns 'proper' to their age and class. I don't use the word as you would, ironically or sarcastically, to denigrate our youngsters aged between twelve and twenty. They are only acting according to their natures, relieved from, or rebelling against, parental control. How should they feel or act differently? If any one is to *blame*, and I think the word has become obsolete – it is surely the parents and grandparents and great-grand-parents, whose nationalism and submissiveness to the dictates of their elders, but not their betters – mark this, James – made possible the two world wars, and may make possible a third.

I don't expect you will agree with any of this, for you have become much more hide-bound by convention than you were, how many years ago?

You clearly don't realize, for instance, that the family-unit is breaking up, and that in a short time it will cease to exist as an active, meaningful element in social life. And yet the last

44

chapter I read, I've forgotten its number, precisely proves my point; here are the two children, Jean and Fergus, adrift in the world, not knowing what is to happen to them, and with little sense of security, except the *money* that, as they vaguely divine, comes to them via Alexey, via Pauline, via Jock and very little love, except what their foster-mother, their paid foster-mother, Mrs. Kirkwood, allows them when her hand has been suitably greased by Jock, via Pauline, via Alexey.

It isn't a pretty story, but my point is that they are *waifs*, with no one to care for them, except Mrs. Kirkwood, whom I suspect of being a venal old hussy, and Jock who kisses and caresses them in the intervals of dancing attendance on Pauline, and her protector. They would be much better looked after, and much happier, in the care of the State, even if their initials, F. for Fergus and J. for Jean, kept them apart for a time. Children are very adaptable – I can see Fergus being quite happy among the male F's, if the sexes have to be discriminated, which I think would be a pity, and Jean still happier among the 'Js', since girls can work out their own happiness much better than boys can. Boys are competitive and envious and emulous and brutal, whereas girls *may* be jealous and unkind, but they have a sympathy and solidarity with each other that boys don't have. The State, with its aim to make our attitudes and be-haviourisms acceptable to each other, would soon cut out these minor differences.

I've told you some of the reasons why I don't like *The Love-Adept*, they are fundamental and grounded on your old-fashioned, almost pre-historic view of life. But there are other smaller defects, mistakes in syntax and grammar, irritating tricks of style, recurrent words and phrases, which I think I should point out. I have marked them lightly in pencil, in my copy, so that you can rub them out before you return the copy to the *Sunday Argus*.

I am returning the book to you, so that you can see my comments, but I beg you to send it on *at once* to the Literary Editor of the *Argus*, who may want to have the book noticed. I have explained to him why *I* cannot, much as I should like to. How I hate doing up parcels! almost as much as I hate undoing them, in that strait-jacket of Sellotape, which breaks one's finger-nails! But I believe you have a 'servant', whom you pay to do this for you.

Incidentally, on some page quite early in the book, occurs the sentence, if sentence it can be called, ('I sometimes forget that my surname is Golightly,' etc.). This is a particularly glaring example of your use, or abuse, of brackets. I often warned you against it in the old days. (It doesn't matter in letters, of course.) (I am parodying your own style.)

'When Alexey first saw Pauline (in the flesh as apart from on the stage) it was – (can you, James, be right about this? Excuse brackets). Would Pauline have had time (or inclination, for that matter) to change into day-clothes and mingle with the audience in the bar? In any professional theatre this would instantly have meant the sack. But according to you, she did. Not everyone recognized her (so changed was she from the virago of the first act), and although she had been murdered everyone in the audience half expected to see her again.

'But Alexey at once recognized her long pale face, her dark hair, and the dark eyebrows which made a wonderful curtain over her blue eyelids, half-obscuring, half-revealing, the indescribable blue-black of her eyes'. (Oh, shades of Stephens' ink, forgive me James, I have dropped into your style, again.) 'He took his courage in both hands, and asked, "Aren't you Miss Pauline Merryweather?" She drew herself up slightly (like one accustomed to impertinent advances from strangers), and replied in a rather deep, tragical voice, "I am, and who are you?" Alexey was slightly ('slightly' is a word you are slightly too fond of, James) taken aback (for in his own walk of life he was used to being recognized and even saluted by porters and commissionaires). But he answered (with a humility that he truly felt) "You wouldn't know me. My name is Alexey, and I have seen you on the stage tonight, and been enchanted by your performance."

'She knew by his voice that he was a gentleman; she could tell by his clothes that he was reasonably well-off, and she answered (moving slightly away from him), (oh dear, 'slightly' again) with great dignity, "I am very glad to have met you, Mr. Alexey, and I hope we shall meet again".'

' "Couldn't we meet again *now*?" he asked, with unaccustomed boldness.

"Now?" she said, looking (and perhaps feeling) slightly (!!) bewildered. "Now?" she repeated, "I don't see," resuming her tragic tone, "why not."

"You were really murdered in the first act?"

She nodded.

"Yes, I'm afraid so. I suppose I deserved it."

"No," said he warmly, "How could you deserve anything so horrible? And it was a mistake on the playwright's part, I know the audience was longing to see you again."

"It is too kind of you to say so, Mr. Alexey."

"Well, may we have a drink to celebrate your deliverance? I don't want to see any more of the play, and perhaps you don't."

('Perhaps', again!).

"I accept with great pleasure, Mr. Alexey."

'He ordered drinks for them both (while the warning for the second act was sounding) and said (raising the glass to his lips), "Here's to your success in this and in your next play".'

'Their eyes met.

' "Amen", she said.'

Well, that is how they 'perhaps', 'slightly', came together.

(In *parenthesis*, James, this sounds like a weak parody of your namesake and master, Henry James.) Of course (as I told you), I don't know what happened afterwards. *Vénus toute entiére à sa proie attachée*, she and her fancy-man, Jock raking in the shekels, while Alexey (idiot that he was – I wish your style wasn't as infectious as influenza) is gradually elbowed out, leaving Pauline and Jock, and Jock's two children possibly, but improbably, sharing the ménage with them, while Alexey, broken-hearted and deserted by them all, decides to commit suicide.

What a bourgeois conclusion!

There are one or two more things I should like to say before thanking you most warmly, for dedicating *The Love-Adept* to me. They are mostly critical, I'm afraid, but in the old days you used to welcome my criticisms, or you said you did.

On page 123, line 3.

'Sometime' for 'some time'. It is an elementary mistake, but not, I think, a mistake often made by writers of your age and experience. When you say, 'sometime ago', Pauline had seemed as anxious to marry him, Alexey, as he had been (and still was) (!) to marry her, you really mean 'some *time*', the emphasis being on *time*, suggesting a definite moment in the past when Pauline, before she met Jock, had this strange idea of marrying Alexey. 'Sometime ago' would mean just any time.

Page 136, line 18, and *passim: who . . . that . . . which . . . what . . .*

You have always been rather shaky on the use of the relative and conjunctive pronoun. Jock, of course, was not an expert on grammar. I admit that the Scotch, or the Scots – if you will have it so, although there is no linguistic justification for this nationalistic variant, are well educated. Do they say in pubs, 'I'll have a wee drop of Scots, or a wee drop of Scottish?' I imagine they ask for a 'double Scotch', I don't know, but you would. What was I going to say? Not butter-Scots, or butter-Scottish. You keep getting in the way of my thoughts. Yes, I admit that the Scotch, man for man, and perhaps woman for woman are better educated than we are. But I don't think that their use of our language, for after all, it *is* our language, makes for elegance. For instance when Jock says to Alexey in an improbable moment of confidence:

' "I don't deny that she" (meaning Pauline) "has in her that which a woman ought to have", he is grammatically correct; and Alexey, instead of telling him that colloquialism has its claims as well as grammar, agrees. His reasons for agreeing are different from the reasons Jock had in commending Pauline.' Jock meant that Pauline had sex and money; Alexey meant by 'that which a woman ought to have', some remote, glamorous attraction, almost Wagnerian in its appeal – a dividend from the *Rheingold* perhaps, quite unmaterialistic.

"That that is is that that is is not that so?"

We used to be given this sentence at school, as a sort of miniature brains-test, and another, 'It was and I said not but'. They made sense if you knew where to put in the commas. Nowadays commas are out of fashion, they are almost taboo, as they are in legal documents, but I think 'that' and 'it' are two of your bug-bears as a stylist, and (that) you should try to keep them under control.

Who cares about style now? But I remember when you did, and *I* still do, though not in my letters, I admit. Let style rip! Even Flaubert let it rip in his letters, which are much nearer to his heart than his considered, over-considered, prose.

But the subject teases me, as a one-time, part-time schoolmistress. Do you remember those days? How far away they seem! – and I can't get out of the habit of thinking that, in writing, *accuracy* is what counts most. If I say, 'the cat sat on the

49

mat', you would know what I mean. It is a statement, perhaps not a very interesting one. But if I say, 'Coming through the garden-door which I believed to have been locked, (as yours often was, in the old days – forgive brackets) into the drawing-room I heard the sound of not many, but a few waters. Like George Robey (do you remember him?) 'I stopped, and I looked and I listened, the sound seemed to come from the ground'. 'It was a gentle rumble, not a roar, and it came from dear Ginger, lying with his paws tucked up under him on the hearth-rug. He was looking *too* sweet.'

This, as no doubt you will recognize, is a quotation from one of the many, many letters, one or two a day? that Alexey wrote to poor Pauline, who was probably in Nottingham, or some such place, in a repertory company, working herself to the bone, and not in the least interested in Alexey's cat, sitting on the mat, but feeling that she must, when she had a moment, make him a suitable reply.

There are other uses or misuses of syntax and grammar that distress me. The word 'like', for instance. 'Like Pauline, she could make herself agreeable if she chose.' This was of a friend of Pauline's, if you remember, whom Pauline tried, or half-tried, to get Alexey interested in, when she was finding him too much of a burden, and Jock too much of an attraction. 'Perhaps' she thought Alexey would subsidize both of them for the sake of keeping in with her. But she didn't succeed, because the friend couldn't make the grade with Alexey, who took no interest in her, and Pauline, naturally, didn't want her to be interested in Jock.

'Unlike Pauline, Calliope' (the friend's stage name) 'pre-ferred her independence to the otiose attentions, however remunerative, of any sugar-daddy.' (Do I detect the influence of Gibbon?)

Surely, James, you *cannot* use 'like' or 'unlike', as a preposition, except in conjunction with the verb 'to be'? 'As was the case with Pauline, she could make herself agreeable if she chose', or 'Calliope was unlike Pauline in that she preferred her independence', etc. 'Like father, like son' is admissible, since no main verb is involved, though I should rather say 'As with father, so with son'. But 'like father, like son' he (Jock) 'like many another half-married man, like Ulysses, for example, liked the off-chance almost as well as the main chance!' Oh dear!

I don't think this is permissible even in a permissive society, and it isn't true of Jock, who seems to have forgotten Gina (or whatever her name was) even while he (rather improbably, *like* I thought) remembered her children.

And there are other things, like split infinitives and sentences ending with a preposition, which seem to show that as far as the art of writing goes, you are determined to be *avant-garde*.

I am grateful to you for dedicating *The Love-Adept* to me, and I only wish I could say I liked it better.

Yours, once,
Elizabeth

P.S. This letter is instead of a review. I thought you would rather hear, even at great length, privately, what I should have felt in conscience bound to write, in brief, publicly.

P.P.S. Just one more thing – your use of, or rather misuse of, the pendent nominative. A substantive with no main verb to follow it! 'Going out to dinner with Jock at the wheel, the Austin Princess did not always behave as it should have.' Are we to understand that the Austin Princess was dining out? How lucky for her; perhaps a manger was provided for her. The A.P. seems to be an important personage in the story, for in another place, page 86, line 3, you write, 'Having purchased this expensive car, Pauline's attitude to Alexey grew appreciably warmer.' One knows what you mean of course; but do the words themselves mean it? How does an attitude purchase an expensive car? Or how does it 'grow warmer' by doing so? The vendors of expensive motor-cars would soon be out of business if a customer could purchase one merely by striking an attitude.

CHAPTER VI

This letter upset James so much while he was reading it that every now and then he put it down, and didn't actually finish it until the next day.

Authors are apt to take praise for granted and to resent even the 'slightest' (a word that Elizabeth III had told him he used too often) breath of criticism. What was wrong with 'slight'? There was no synonym for it. 'Mild' might do; a 'mild' attack of jaundice was equivalent to a 'slight' attack of jaundice (if jaundice could be 'slight'). 'The 'mildest' breath of criticism': that was a true equivalent, that met the case. No, *that* met the case: how right Elizabeth was to say he couldn't control the word 'that'. Besides, 'mild' had so many extra meanings: a 'mild' man (such as he was) could not be equated with a 'slight' man, which he knew he was not, physically, for he weighed 13 stone, nor, he hoped, in its more archaic usage, meaning a man of no importance, a man to be disregarded, a poor fellow. A 'mild' day meant something: a 'slight' day meant nothing.

He didn't mind being teased, he rather liked it, but he minded being made fun of – who doesn't? And Elizabeth III, with her ex-schoolmistressy gift of making a pupil feel small, had reduced him to the level of a schoolboy, with a schoolboy's diffidence and need of reassurance.

She had made him dissatisfied with his vocabulary, and what was a writer without a vocabulary? It was her criticisms of his use of English that rankled; they rankled even more than her general strictures of his book. They rankled more than 'slightly' and although he knew she was paying off an old score, they still rankled.

His first impulse was to write Elizabeth III an indignant letter defending *The Love-Adept* and asking her how she could presume to judge it when she had only read as far as the chapter, less than half-way through, when the children are talking to each other. Then he remembered the adage:

> Till you know your feelings better,
> Do not post that angry letter.

So he desisted; for it was as ignominious to try to defend one's work against hostile criticism as it would be to defend one's own child. James was a bachelor; but if he had been a married man with children, and a friend had told him that they were one and all ugly and badly-behaved, he wouldn't have tried to defend them, singly or collectively. It was too undignified. All he could say would be: 'You may not like them, but I happen to'.

And besides the insult (for one's books were, in a sense, one's children, and more intimately an extension and projection of oneself than children often were) there remained the disquieting thought, 'Suppose Elizabeth III was *right*? Suppose *The Love-Adept* was a bad book, and in telling him so she had written in good faith?' He had assumed that her object, in denigrating it, was a sort of tit-for-tat: 'You hurt me once, and I'll hurt you now'. But it might not have been: it wasn't beyond the bounds of possibility that she genuinely disliked the book. She had certainly given adequate reasons for disliking it: its similarity, in theme at any rate, to *Lady Chatterley's Lover* was only one. Perhaps it *was* badly written, with the brackets she so much disliked, but which she herself had succumbed to, saying they were permissible in a letter. And the misuse of 'like', and the 'pendent nominatives', and the confusions between 'that' and 'who' and 'which'. Regarded objectively, she was quite an acute critic, or the *Sunday Argus* wouldn't have kept her on so long. What a pity they had.

And the fact that she hadn't been able to finish the book, which he had at first thought invalidated her condemnation of it – if she was writing from her critical perceptions and not from her wounded heart – wasn't that enough to damn it?

James writhed in his chair. Why was it that a few words of dispraise from Elizabeth III caused him so much pain, whereas the appreciation that Elizabeths I and II had shown, didn't correspondingly please him. Was the balance of life weighed in favour of suffering? Perhaps it was; the Buddhists, someone had told him, believed that existence *was* suffering.

For one reason or another, none of the Elizabeths had been able to finish the book – a fact that couldn't be ignored, although the first two gave convincing reasons for not being in at the death. 'Very few there are, and those few very weary, who are in at the death of the Blatant Beast'. This, or words to the same effect, was one of Macaulay's comments on Spenser's *Faerie Queene*. It was a notorious critical 'howler', and showed that Macaulay was an unconscientious and irresponsible reader, for the Blatant Beast did not die. And, to turn from great things to small, how mistaken Elizabeth III had been in her prevision of the ending of *The Love-Adept*. She condemned the book on many grounds, but above all for the triteness of its ending, although she had no idea, except in her own mind, what that ending was going to be.

How conceited some people were!

James started to write a letter to her. This will take the skin off her nose, he thought. But after a time he put down his pen. Why recriminate with an old friend, when you haven't many left?

Calm down, calm down, relax, as they said nowadays, and re-read the chapter, which Elizabeth III had chosen for special disapproval. James hated re-reading his books: it seemed to touch a sore spot in him. How could he have thought like that, written like that, been like that – that sort of person? (Elizabeth III wouldn't have approved of all those 'thats'.) Was one's past personality as 'evinced' (as Emily Brontë might have said) in one's work, something, someone, whom one cordially disliked? One couldn't get away from the fact that one was, or had been, somewhere in one's books – the presiding spirit, the evil genius! And to meet this spirit again, so like one's own, but oh so different! – was a disturbing experience. All the same, it must be faced.

True to her word, Elizabeth had sent him back her advance review copy of *The Love-Adept*, with its pencilled scrawlings, which were like deliberate exercises in defacement. He found the offending chapter; it was less than half way through the book. India-rubber in hand, and trying to stifle his distaste, he set about eliminating her wounding comments. In vain, in vain: they remained as clear on the creased and crumpled pages as they were to his own mind. Just one thing he succeeded in deleting, and for that he took his pen: the dedication, 'To Elizabeth'.

'I must ask my publisher to send the *Sunday Argus* another review copy,' he thought.

.   .   .

Why did Elizabeth III particularly dislike this particular chapter in The Love-Adept? A breath of outside criticism means more, in the way of suffering, to an author than a gale of self-criticism. None the less, he must try to find out what she meant; and here the chapter was.

'When is Dad coming to see us again?' asked Fergus.

'Oh, I don't know,' his sister answered. 'Dad's like that, he often goes away. He has to, it's his job.'

They were sitting side by side on two rather uncomfortable chairs in Mrs. Kirkwood's front room. The one easy chair she reserved for herself, and didn't encourage them, although she didn't forbid them, to use. And it was the same with the sofa, which was en suite with the chair. It was for special occasions, not just for young children to sit on.

She was a kind-hearted and a just woman, and she was being paid – sufficiently paid – to take care of them, and she knew what was due to her, and due to them. Happily for her and for them she liked children, being a widow with none of her own, but she didn't mean to spoil them, and was cautious of investing too much affection, and still more too much money in them, for how could she tell how long a man of Jock's migratory habits, and uncertain tendencies, would last? Garage-hands, lorry-drivers, they were here today and gone to-morrow. You couldn't keep track of them. A Scotsman was more reliable than an Englishman; but supposing Jock buzzed off in his car (or in Mr. Alexey's car or in anybody's car) and left the children on her hands: what then? He seemed to have a good job with this Miss Pauline, but she, being an actress, was just as unreliable as he, and would their connection last?

'He hasn't been away so long before without coming to see us,' said Fergus plaintively. 'It's nine days, five hours and seven minutes.' He looked at the clock on the chimney piece.

'Not to worry,' said Jean, with her grown-up air, 'Dad's not like Mum, he's sure to come back.'

'You said Mum would come back,' said Fergus, 'but she didn't.'

He sounded tearful, and wanting to reassure him Jean said, 'Now don't think about it too much. Granny Kirkwood will be coming with our tea in a few minutes.'

'Eight and a half minutes,' said Fergus who, like many small boys, was acutely time-conscious. 'Wouldn't it be a surprise if Dad came in just when Granny did – just in time for tea. Dad likes his tea – Granny would be sure to give him a cup of tea.'

'Oh yes, she would,' said Jean, 'and she might give him a drop of whisky with it, he likes whisky in his tea.'

Fergus shook his head.

'Not when he's driving.'

'Oh, a wee drappie wouldn't matter. You're always so afraid of things.'

'But do you think he really loves us?'

'Has he ever hit you?' asked Jean.

'Only about twice.'

'Well he wouldn't hit you if he didn't love you.'

'Has he ever hit you, Jean?'

'No, men never hit girls, even fathers don't! That doesn't prove anything.'

'But he's been away so long,' said Fergus with a quaver in his voice. 'He's never been away so long before. Suppose he stayed away for ever? What would happen to us then? Granny Kirkwood wouldn't take care of us if she wasn't paid to. A real Granny might, but she's not our real Granny, I know that, besides, you told me.'

'She's better than some people's real grannies,' Jean answered, 'and better than some mothers, too. Our Mum just left. She put a note in pencil on a bit of toilet paper, on the table with the broken leg where she kept her make-up things, saying 'I've quit,' and that was all. You and I were sleeping together in the small bed, Dad and Mum used to sleep in the big one. I don't know how grown-up people sleep, but he didn't notice that she wasn't there. You didn't

wake up because nothing can wake you, once you are asleep. I didn't
wake up while she was putting her things into her suit-case – she
must have been as quiet as a mouse – and she didn't turn the light on,
so she must have got it all ready before, but I heard the door shut,
ever so softly, like a sound in a dream, and I lay awake for a long
time before I went to sleep again. And you know what happened
after that!

'I know that Mum didn't come back, and Dad tried to find her, and
couldn't.'

'No, she took a car from another garage, Reynolds' it was. I heard
it ticking away on the road, but I never guessed it had anything to do
with us. Of course Dad comes back at any old hour when he's got a
job on, but it couldn't be him, because there he was in bed – he takes
up so much room in bed – you know that because you've slept with
him when Mum was away, and someone else was in our bed, some
wee lassie, I forget who.'

'That was before Mr. Alexey came to be friends with us – we have
a bed each now,' said Fergus, rather proudly. 'And Dad has a bed to
himself too. I always hope I shall wake up and see him in it.'

'Oh, you will, you will,' his sister told him consolingly. 'He'll
come back, never fear.'

But Fergus wouldn't be convinced.

'I don't see why. He may have forgotten all about us, just like
Mum did. She never told us she was going to leave us, and she was
our Mum, and he's only our Dad, which isn't half as much, really.'

'You always look on the dark side,' his sister said impatiently, but
there was a tremor of doubt in her voice which Fergus didn't fail to
notice.

'If Dad couldn't pay for us, or didn't want to, would Granny
Kirkwood still look after us, or should we be sent away to a Detention
Centre?'

'Detention Centre! What do you mean? Only bad children go to
Detention Centres. We haven't done anything bad – not really bad.

You have done some bad things, like all boys do. You stole some of Mrs. McGregor's apples, and were sick afterwards because they weren't ripe, do you remember? They were as green as grass. But they wouldn't send you to a Detention Centre just for doing that. If they tried to I should scream and scream, I should scream the house down, oh yes, I should. And I should say we were children of a Broken Home, which is quite true, seeing that Mum ran away with her boy-friend – and then they couldn't do anything to us, anything bad – because we come from a Broken Home.'

'But what would happen to us?' insisted Fergus. 'Where shall we go if Granny Kirkwood turns us out? There aren't any homes for good children.'

'There may be, Fergie darling. It's just that we don't know about them.'

Her brother shook his head – it was his commonest gesture, as if he was chronically denying the possibility of good fortune. But he tried to ward off his forebodings, and said, on a note of doubtful hope,

'Do you think Miss Pauline (I can't remember her other name) would she be our Mum, now that our Mum's gone?'

Jean considered this: oddly enough, it was a new thought to her.

'Do you mean that Dad and Miss Pauline might get married?'

'Well, not married, because Dad's married already – but wed, there's a difference, isn't there?'

It was Jean's turn to shake her head. 'I don't think so. Married and wed, they both mean the same. You can't get married unless you've been divorced.'

'But heaps of people get married without being divorced!'

Jean was annoyed at being caught out in such an unsophisticated remark.

'Of course they do, you silly! But only when they haven't been married before. Dad has been married before, and perhaps Miss Pauline has – we don't know.'

'But she's called Miss Pauline – somebody.'

'Oh, that makes no difference on the stage. On the stage they call themselves Miss or Mrs. just as it takes their fancy, and the men are all Mister, so you can't tell whether they are married or not.'

Fergus then asked the question which had been occupying his mind for some time.

'Do you think our Dad might wed Miss Pauline, or Mrs. Pauline even if he didn't marry her?'

Glad to get her own back on Fergus for having scored off her conversationally, Jean said:

'He couldn't be married to them both, you silly! No, I don't think she would marry him.'

Fergus looked disappointed.

'Why not? She's always going about with him, and the last time they came here they kissed each other, twice, no, three times.'

'That doesn't mean anything,' said Jean. 'I've only been to the theatre now and then, when Dad took us to see Miss Pauline, and she was always kissing somebody.'

'It didn't mean she was in love with them?' asked Fergus.

'Of course not. How could you be in love with somebody you'd only met on the stage?'

'You could be,' persisted Fergus. 'Dad only met Miss Pauline at the garage, and he fell in love with her at once. And so did she, with him. I like her very much. I wish she was our Mum.'

'Well, you can wish,' replied Jean, reasserting her elder-sisterly authority, 'you can wish, but I can tell you one thing: it won't happen.'

'Why not?' answered Fergus, argumentative though still tearful. 'When she came here before with Dad, she said, 'You are both little darlings, and I love you.' 'You heard her say it, Jean.'

Jean admitted that she had heard. 'But it doesn't mean anything. It's something they say on the stage' – she tried to imitate a refined voice, 'May little darlings, I loave you.' Why should she loave us?

It sounded suspiciously like *loathe*, but that word wasn't in the children's vocabulary.

'Because she loves Dad,' said Fergus, 'and we belong to him, don't we?'

The question hung in the air until Jean, leaning forward until her lips almost touched her brother's ear, said, 'I want to tell you something. Would you like to hear?'

There was a faint threat in her voice, and Fergus said, 'Yes, no, yes, no. Yes, please tell me, Jean.'

'It's Mr. Alexey that Pauline's really in love with, not Dad.'

Fergus was quite overcome, and the interpretation of the situation he had been building up in his mind went hay-wire.

'Mr. Alexey? I've only seen him once or twice, but he's old and ugly.'

'He may be,' said his sister, 'but if you ask me, it's he who runs the show.'

'What show?' asked Fergus, bewildered.

'Oh, the whole set-up,' said Jean, negligently. 'The way they all three go about together. I suppose you imagine that the Austin Princess is Miss Pauline's?'

'I thought it was Dad's as a matter of fact,' said Fergus, humbly.

'Well, as a matter of fact it isn't,' said Jean sharply. 'How could Dad afford a car like that? He couldn't afford to run it, let alone own it. Nor could Miss Pauline, from what I've heard.'

Fergus was aware of a gulf opening at his feet.

'What have you heard?'

'I couldn't help hearing,' said Jean, obliquely and obscurely, 'because Mr. Alexey was talking to Granny Kirkwood in the kitchen. And he said, "Put all the expenses down to me, Mrs. Kirkwood." And Granny, who's always rather hot about money, said "Who's paying for the car? They know at the garage that Jock isn't. They were quite unpleasant about it." '

'What did Mr. Alexey say?'

'He said, "Mrs. Merryweather, of course. Mrs. Merryweather is a friend of mine, and if necessary we share the expenses." So you see.'

'I don't see,' said Fergus. 'Why should Mr. Alexey pay for Miss Pauline's car? Do you mean he pays for everything, you and me, and Dad, and Miss Pauline?'

'I think he does,' said Jean.

'But why? Is he so fond of us all? And perhaps he'd like some children of his own,' Fergus went on lugubriously. 'We aren't his real children, any more than Granny Kirkwood is our real Granny.'

'He's too old,' said Jean decisively. 'He must be 45, if he's a day, and men can't have children at that age, even if they wanted them. If he'd wanted children of his own, he'd have had them before now.'

'But he isn't married,' objected Fergus.

'That doesn't make any difference, silly,' said Jean. 'Men don't have to be married.'

At that moment they heard a call from within, a warm vibrant voice. 'Come along, children, tea's ready.' They had all their meals in the kitchen, but were sometimes allowed to sit in the front room, to be out of the way.

Tea-time is a happy time, especially for children, and Mrs. Kirkwood did not stint her charges' appetites. Scones, and cakes, and bread and butter, and jam. They were so taken up, first with the eye-catching, breath-taking allure of these delicacies, and then by tucking into them, that they didn't open their mouths, except to take in food, for several minutes.

'Well, what sort of a day have you had?' asked Mrs. Kirkwood, when the sounds of the munching and swallowing had begun to die down. 'School, eh? and then school again, eh? Which of you did best?'

'None of us did best,*' snapped Jean, rather crushingly, between bites. 'We all do well, of course, but none of us does* best. *That wouldn't be right.'*

'Why not?' asked Mrs. Kirkwood. 'It was right in my day. And please don't talk with your mouth full.'

'I can't talk with it empty, when I am eating, can I?' said Jean, eyeing another cake.

'Fergus doesn't talk with his mouth full,' Mrs. Kirkwood replied, not unnaturally wishing to drive a wedge between brother and sister.

Fergus looked up, half pleased at Granny's approval, half fearful of what might come next.

'That's because he has nothing to say,' said Jean. 'He doesn't speak, he only answers.'

'I wish there were more like him,' said Mrs. Kirkwood, with a sigh. Fergus was her favourite, and Jean was well aware of it, or she wouldn't have criticized him in Granny Kirkwood's presence.

'Speech is silver, but silence is golden,' said Mrs. Kirkwood, giving Jean a look. 'It's a good thing to know when to hold one's

tongue, isn't it, Fergus? My husband never did, that's why the landlord of the local refused to serve him, on more than one occasion. Whisky made him antagonistic, and people didn't like it. And they didn't like him standing with his back to the bar, instead of facing it, as all ordinary mortals do. You wouldn't understand that, either of you, and I hope you never will – I sincerely hope not. You don't want to start a fight, do you? You couldn't now, you're much too young to go into a pub, unless it's an off licence, and somebody has given you the money to buy a pint of beer or it might even be a bottle of Scotch for somebody. Teacher's preferably.'

Mrs. Kirkwood sighed again, and having digested her own thoughts, amid a respectful silence on Fergus's part, and an impatient one on Jean's, she recollected herself, and said to Jean,

'What was I going to ask you?'

'I can't remember, Granny. It was such a long time ago, and anyhow how could I know what you meant to ask us?'

Mrs. Kirkwood poured herself another cup of tea, and searched her mind.

'Oh, it was to do with school. You said all did well, but no one did best.'

'Yes, Gran, because it would make the others jealous.'

'Don't call me Gran, I don't like it, and besides I'm only your Granny in name, and because Jock wants me to be. As for jealousy, you can't get anywhere without being jealous. You just let the rest drive over you, as men-drivers drive over women-drivers. Jock now, your Dad, he's a considerate man, as men go, and a good friend to me. But how often have I heard him say, because he doesn't mince his words (thank God you don't take after him in that, and I wouldn't let you anyhow), 'those damned women-drivers are a perfect menace on the roads.'

'Do you think he's jealous of lady-drivers?' asked Fergus, timidly.

'No, what call has he to be jealous? But he is jealous, just because

65

he's a man, and all men are jealous. If they see another man getting
ahead of them, on the roads or anywhere else, they go quite dotty.'

'But aren't women jealous too, Granny?'

Mrs. Kirkwood hesitated. She always treated Fergus's questions
more seriously than she treated Jean's, and not only because they were
rarer.

'Well, yes, they are, Fergus, but in a different way. You wouldn't
understand.'

Encouraged to proceed, Fergus asked,

'Is Dad jealous?'

Mrs. Kirkwood looked at him. She was never averse from discussing
human relationships, even with a child.

'No, who's he got to be jealous of? Your Mum's gone off with
that nigger, worse luck, though it's good luck really, and I don't care
who hears me say it.'

'Couldn't he be jealous of Mr. Alexey?'

Mrs. Kirkwood allowed a slight note of admiration to creep into her
voice. [James, reading, frowned. Too late to cut out 'slight'.]

'You're a sharp one, aren't you? No, he's not jealous of Mr.
Alexey, if you ask me.'

'Why not, Granny? They're always going about together, and he
sometimes kisses her.'

'Who kisses who?'

'Mr. Alexey sometimes kisses Miss Pauline, but Dad never
does.'

'Oh, that's because he's driving. You can't kiss someone when
you're driving, not safely, even your Dad couldn't, though he's a
good driver. Besides, they always sit in the back seat.'

'But couldn't you kiss somebody in the back seat?'

'Not if you were the driver.'

'But he could kiss her?'

'You muddle me so with all this kissing, but I see what you mean.
Yes, Mr. Alexey could kiss her.'

'*And wouldn't Dad be jealous?*'

'*Oh, you've got jealousy on the brain. Your Dad is just their driver and they don't pay him to kiss anybody. He has plenty to do without that. Now finish up your tea. And you too, Jean. You've been staring in front of you like a famished angel.*'

'*I was thinking of what happened when Miss Pauline sits in the* front *seat. She does, sometimes, you know.*'

'*You* are *observant, to use an old-fashioned expression,*' Mrs. Kirkwood said, getting up and beginning to clear away the tea-things. '*I don't know why you youngsters think so much about sex. We never did, in our day, and it isn't healthy. Good Lord, what was that?*'

The door bell buzzed a second time; they hadn't heard it before.

'*Now, be good children,*' said Mrs. Kirkwood, '*and wash up the tea-cups and I'll go and see who it is. It may be nobody, but if it is somebody, I'll let them through into the front room, and you can come too, if you wash your hands and tidy yourselves. There, there, and there,*' she said, indicating with rapid gestures where the tea-things were to go. '*And mind you don't break anything, Fergus. I have my good name to think of, even if you haven't.*'

She bustled out, and Jean and Fergus, well-used to the kitchen routine, went to work with might and main, hoping they would be asked into the front room.

'*Careful, careful, Fergus.*'

'*I am* being *careful, Jean.*'

Swish. swish.

'*It may not be anybody, but do straighten your hair, Fergus, and look at your tie, it's all askew.*'

'*I can't look at it,*' protested Fergus, '*while I'm washing up.*'

'*I suppose not,*' said Jean, going to the looking-glass and giving herself a pat or two. '*Boys are always so helpless. But she might have told us,*' she added, smoothing down her hair in one place, and

c*   67

ruffling it in another. 'You look awful, Fergus, but it doesn't really matter how boys look.'

'Perhaps it isn't anybody,' said Fergus hopefully. 'Perhaps it's only the man who collects the rent.'

'I hope it will be somebody,' said his more socially-disposed sister. 'I hope it will be somebody, or anybody. Sh!' and she waved aloft a warning tea-towel.

Voices and shuffling sounds in the passage came through to the kitchen. When they were hushed the door opened dramatically, and Mrs. Kirkwood's face shone through, so transformed and rejuvenated by the excitement of hostess-ship that it was hardly recognizable.

'Come along,' she said in a piercing whisper, 'it's them!'

CHAPTER VII

James pushed the book aside, keeping his finger in the place.
Why did Elizabeth III dislike this chapter so much? He
had enjoyed writing it, more indeed, than he had enjoyed
writing most of the other chapters. What was wrong with
it?

Elizabeth III, in her long diatribe – some of which he had
committed to memory, and some of which, in a temper he had
erased – was critical of his use of the verb 'begin'. 'It is nearly
always redundant,' she said, 'Why write', "Jean and Fergus
began to feel frightened when they thought what might
happen if?" All we want to know is that they felt frightened.
Again you say Jock was "beginning" to lose his hair: an
ambiguous expression any way; it might mean, in the vernacular, that Jock was losing his temper. Or again on p. 166 line 3
when something happened which I really *don't* want to know
about. There are beginnings and there are endings, of course.
"In the beginning was the Word and the Word was with God,
and the Word was God" – Well, we know where we
are. But when you say, "Jock began to wonder if his relationship with Pauline would stay the course," surely it would
have been better to say, *tout court*, "Jock wondered if his
relationship with P. would stay the course?" We are not
interested in how something began – are you interested in
how a cold *began*? – but we may want to know how it
ended.

'Page 165, line 9, which I glanced at before I decided to put the book down: "Pauline and Alexey and Jock were beginning to take each other for granted, when –" Why not, were taking each other for granted?'

At once James began to see (but why 'began' to see?) that many things were wrong. 'At once he *saw*. . . .' He didn't *know* what an establishment like Mrs Kirkwood's who let a room for lodgers (or was it two rooms?) was really like. He had tried to portray her as mercenary and the children as cynical, to suit what he believed to be the modern taste, but had he overdone it, in one direction or another? Was Granny Kirkwood too mercenary, or not mercenary enough? Were the children too cynical, or not cynical enough? Was the whole Kirkwood set-up too sentimental, or not sentimental enough? Too sentimental, he thought most people would say, but after all, there was still sentiment about, especially among Scottish widows, with no children of their own. At least, being a novelist, he could pretend there was.

And why make the whole situation unrelievedly brutal, as though all goodness and kindness had disappeared from the world – even if it had, and been swept away by mechanical brooms sweeping and cleansing the corridors of power?

If only Elizabeth III had told him exactly *what* she disliked in this chapter, it would have been more helpful – if she had even said 'you don't know what you are writing about!' it would have been more helpful. In fact, all she had done was to make him deeply dissatisfied with what he had written, and deeply distrustful of anything he might write.

He had finished re-reading the chapter, but he could easily anticipate her criticisms of the remainder. 'This triangular situation, James, that you have contrived and . . . and concocted, this ill-matched trio is not only unrepresentative of life as we know it, it is quite untrue to life.'

'That I deny, Elizabeth, I deny it absolutely. I could give you at least three examples – since trios run in your mind – of situations in all essentials similar to the one I tried to describe. I have never been involved in one myself, so I don't know what it *feels* like; but I can assure you that they have existed, do exist, and will go on existing. You may say '*aut enim*' (as Cicero used to say, when anticipating the objections of an opposing advocate), 'you may say that the Pauline-Alexey-Jock imbroglio doesn't correspond to the normal pattern of social attitudes. It may not correspond, but it constantly occurs, it is not a *hapax legomenos* (you wouldn't understand what that means, it means a single exception). It happens, as I said before, quite often, and more often than it used to, because the changing structure of society makes such irregular relationships more possible and more probable, and more permissible. They weren't probable, though they weren't impossible, fifty or sixty years ago, when Strindberg wrote *Mademoiselle Julie*. *Then* it shocked people that a well-born girl should fall in love with a footman: it wouldn't shock people now. Footmen may be a dying race, but they have their counterparts in other walks of life. There are still well-to-do men like Alexey, who attach themselves hopelessly but whole-heartedly to stars of the second magnitude like Pauline (who still exist too, forgive brackets). And there are still good-looking working-men who attract some women, though by no means all. Women are much less susceptible to personal beauty in men than men are to personal beauty in women, otherwise Jock's wife wouldn't have run away with a Negro, although he may have been good-looking too: some women are 'kinky' about Negroes. I can't say much more, dear Elizabeth, because I am in the dark as to what you *really* dislike in the book, and I feel I am fighting a shadow-battle. You have told me I am not 'with it', or that I am a 'square', or some such discredited geometrical figure; but it may have nothing to do with that, it may just be that you

don't like my figure – not my *shape*, for that was never anything to boast of – but *some* part of me.

> The reason why I cannot tell
> But this I know, I know full well,
> I do not like thee, Dr. Fell.

'Your strictures (I don't take the grammatical ones too
seriously, for everyone has his or her own way of writing.):
le style c'est l'homme, or in your case, *la femme*; you would
agree to that, wouldn't you? – no insult intended, for more and
more women write well. And you have been a fiction-critic
for how long – twenty years? Not the experience of a lifetime,
as Whistler said, but long enough to know what you are
talking about. If only I knew exactly *what* you are talking
about! It may not be something in my book, it may be something in *me*, that you find unsatisfactory.'

Tired of this long soliloquy, or rather this duologue with
Elizabeth III's shade, James tried to stifle it. It might form the
substance of the letter he must write to her, and then again,
it mightn't. He didn't want to show her how she had hurt
him, both as a novelist and a man. But write to her he
must.

Damn her! She had left him on such bad terms with himself
that he didn't know what to do next. Tidy his desk? Rearrange
his pictures? Write some letters? Make a telephone-call to one
of the other Elizabeths, who might restore his *amour-propre*?
But no, they wouldn't, because he had had to confess to them
that the book hadn't been dedicated to them, and they would
be bound to feel hurt – what woman, or what man, for that
matter, wouldn't feel hurt at having a proffered present
snatched away from them? Even the Gods cannot recall their
gifts, and he was far from being a god – but not far from being
a fool. What a fool he had been not to send a proof-copy of

The Love-Adept to Elizabeth IV, and ask her if she liked it enough to accept the dedication.

There had been several objections to this course, none of which, now, seemed valid, or 'viable', to use a more contemporary expression. Yes, Elizabeth III, 'viable.'

One was the time-factor. His publisher had sent him two copies of *The Love-Adept* in page-proof (nowadays they seldom sent an author galleys), with instructions to return the proof instantly, otherwise the publication of the book might be delayed for several months, in fact postponed from their Autumn to their Spring List, if not for ever.

How extraordinary! He couldn't find anywhere one of the six complimentary copies of *The Love-Adept* that his publisher had sent him. Four had gone to the four Elizabeths; one he had given to someone else, he couldn't remember whom; but the sixth copy, that he had meant to keep for himself, had vanished.

Never mind, there was still the duplicate of the printer's proof copy. It lacked the printers' corrections, and suggestions, scratched, like wounds, in thin red ink: still it would be sufficient: it would give the substance of the book.

Of course, the proof was valueless now: whatever could be done, had been done. All the same, his first feelings when confronted by it, came back to him. He was very susceptible to any kind of pressure, especially when a dead-line, such as catching a train, was imposed. Moreover he was a slow and inaccurate proof-reader, and when he found himself confronted by a page-proof, he was beside himself. A page-proof in which a word or two crossed out must be replaced by a word or two of the same length, gave him the feeling of claustrophobia one doubtless gets in a strait-jacket.

He pounced, almost in a panic, on the printer's proof. Here was the first misprint, 'Alexey thought he had money to turn.' How odd that misprints should so often be funny, as if some demon had entered the compositor's mind, ridiculing the sentence. At any rate it was easy to turn 'turn' into 'burn'. But how about this one, which the printer himself had queried, in thin red ink: 'He (Jock) had his hiving to make, and it didn't matter much to him how or where he behived, so long as he could make a good hiving for himself and the children that Gina had bestowed on him? One hive was very much like another; whether the honey, the bee-all and the end-all, came from Pauline, the queen-bee, or from Alexey, his successful suitor in the nuptial flight?' And who was bee, anyhow?

Oh, the dangers of metaphor! It had been a real headache to straighten this one out.

If James had not been so acutely conscious of the pressure of time he would have sent the spare copy, with all its damaging misprints and errors, to Elizabeth IV, and asked her whether she would accept the dédicace, in which case he could have inscribed both her name and surname on the title-page, and there would have been none of this confusion.

But if she didn't like the book, if she liked it as little as Elizabeth III liked it, or even less, if she had had time to make up her mind, before the time-driven copy went to the printer, could she have said 'No'? No, she couldn't, and it was this consideration, more than any other, which induced James to give her the book with its semi-anonymous dedication, and a covering note, explaining.

But of course, as he now saw, being a sensible woman whose mind was quickly made up, she would have had no difficulty in saying 'yes' or 'no'.

He had attached far too much importance to the dedication. What *did* it matter? If John Milton had dedicated *Paradise Lost* to Satan (as he well might have) Satan would probably have been quite pleased.

So why? –

James was in the mood, common to other folk as well as to authors, when everything he had ever done seemed to be wrong – misguided, mistaken, the result of an unbalanced judgement, of taking himself, and other people, too seriously. What is a book? It comes out, it is read for a month or two, and is forgotten. Elizabeth IV might find some pretext for not reading *The Love-Adept* to the end, just as her co-Elizabeths had.

All the same, life has to go on, and one cannot willingly acquiesce in frustration, for a year, a month, or even a day.

James tramped up and down his room with an eye to possible improvements. Everything, the pictures, the book-cases, the rugs, looked as wrong, as wrong in themselves, and in their relations to each other, as if they had been seen through the eyes of Elizabeth III. The most distasteful of all, the one he could hardly bear to face, was the proof copy of *The Love-Adept*. But like many other distasteful things and objects, which we would gladly shun, it was the one that most clamorously claimed his attention. It was as unwelcome, as difficult to feel pleased or happy with, as a child recently expelled from school, and on its way to Borstal. All the same, he had a parent's responsibility for it. Parents were held responsible for everything in these days: the sins of the children were visited on their parents unto the third and fourth generation of those who had begotten them.

CHAPTER VIII

James tried to see what was wrong with the offending chapter, or more wrong with it than with the other chapters. The timing was quite good: it showed the Pauline-Alexey-Jock ménage at its peak of success, with each member of the trio apparently in tune with the others. Moreover, it presented them instead of analysing them, as he had been apt to do in earlier chapters.

How quickly you can analyse a character away! A word from him, *in propria persona*, counts for more than a hundred words about him, strained through the filter of the author's mind.

The mind directs, but the subconscious mind suggests. Its suggestions are more fruitful to a work of art than the mind's directions; but without the mind's directions, what a quagmire we should get into! It would be a road without sign-posts, a fast road but without a destination.

Then the children, so James felt or hoped, came to life as they had never done when they were the shadowy, hinted-at encumbrances on the grown-ups' path to bliss. They were aware that they had a life to lead, and a part to play, even if they didn't know what it was. Mrs. Kirkwood knew the lie of the land; she wasn't born yesterday, as they were, poor wee things. But even she didn't know where they were all heading for, or when the break would come (for she felt it must come), or where to turn for the next penny, supposing Pauline and Alexey fell out, and left Jock in the lurch. Jock would stick to them no doubt, as he had before this strange windfall came his way; but would he be able to keep them, and her, in the comfort that they now enjoyed? She was a soft-hearted woman, but hard-headed, too; she had to think of herself, and the probable decline in her standard of living. She might have to look for other lodgers, less trouble than the children were, and better able to pay than Jock would be without the aid of Alexey's fancy-woman. Pauline's fancy-man.

She wanted to know how she stood, but how could she find out? She was as quick as anyone to see which way the wind lay, and she thought she knew: Alexey, mild-mannered as he was, submissive as he seemed to be, held the purse-strings: he paid the piper, and it was he who, ultimately, would call the tune. Jock would find himself out on his ear (redundant, Elizabeth III, if you like that better) he might be able to afford the small back room for his children and himself, when he was reduced to working as a garage-hand; but not the big front room: oh, no. Where was the money to come from? That was the all-important question.

A thing James wanted to point out, and which he thought he had pointed out, was that although many, perhaps most people's motives were cynical, especially where money was concerned, their behaviour, very often was not. Jean and Fergus were not too young to have an axe to grind, and they knew which side their bread was buttered; so did Mrs. Kirkwood, so did Pauline know, and Alexey knew (he it was who provided the butter), and perhaps more than any of them, Jock knew. Yet when they were all in the same room together (admittedly Pauline's contingent made a very brief call), they all behaved, in their various ways, as if each other's welfare was the one thing they had at heart.

You, no doubt, Elizabeth Chillingsworth, Elizabeth III,

would say that this couldn't be so, and that people's behaviour is in keeping with the pattern of their thoughts. You may be right: and I can't discuss it with you, because you never told me what you thought was wrong with the chapter, and you never bothered to finish the book.

If Elizabeth III had meant James to have these imaginary conversations with her shade, and torment him by guessing why she had formed such an unfavourable opinion of his book, she had certainly succeeded.

And then it suddenly struck him, was her singling out of this chapter for especial condemnation just a ruse: poke the animal, and see how it will react? It could be: it could be a way of paying off an old score. She knew how sensitive he was to criticism, she knew that one hostile word weighed more with him than a hundred words of praise. Perhaps she only said she disliked it to have her revenge by making him dissatisfied with the whole book.

Ah yes, ah yes! It might be so, it might be so. It was a plausible theory and ministered to his self-esteem. But the seed of doubt, once sown, grows up like the mustard-tree, and the fowls of the air lodge in the branches thereof, and nothing will flourish underneath.

But he must make some acknowledgment of her letter. It couldn't be thanks. Nor could it be a defence of his book, based on the imaginary conversations with her that still repeated themselves in his mind. One can defend oneself from attack, because one is a person, an individual, a human being, compact of mind, and heart, of nerves, and bones, and blood. A person is an organism, living, developing, dwindling and dying, not to be judged by standards of aesthetic criticism as a work of art is, for however much the standards of criticism may change, they always have an ideal standard of art in view.

Dear Elizabeth,

Thank you for your letter acknowledging receipt of my novel, *The Love-Adept*, and making various criticisms of that novel in particular, and of my work in general, my use and misuse of certain words and phrases, and my mistakes of grammar and syntax (I am never quite sure which is which, please forgive brackets).

As you will realize, having been yourself in the book business for so many years, it is quite impossible for me, at this late hour, to act upon your suggestions and admonitions. But I have noted them carefully, in case I should ever write another novel.

The conscious mind is often a barrier to imaginative writing, which is one reason why some novelists are heavy drinkers, for drink is almost always a gateway to (though not always a gateway from) the subconscious mind. But one can't do without the conscious mind: the construction of the book depends on it, the strategy and tactics of the book depend on it, and so, in a lesser degree, do the grammar and the syntax.

The *nominativi pendentes* (is that the correct form of the plural?) I feel I can weed out for myself. There shall be no more sentences such as, 'Jock having carefully cleaned the car, for Pauline liked to see it bright and shining, although Alexey, its owner, didn't mind, it began to rain.' I agree that that sentence is a *disaster*, and it also illustrates how the word 'it', such a small word, but an evil imp, is always tripping me up. I can never make 'it' clear what 'it' refers to.

How much easier to write in French (if one *could* write in French – again forgive brackets, I have an incurably parenthetical bent). The French language, I am told, and my 'slight' acquaintance with 'it' bears this out, although perhaps less rich in *nuances* than ours is, is also much more precise. The French range of expression may be more limited than ours, but 'it' is always clear what Monsieur or Madame or Mademoiselle *means*. ('What then does Cardinal Newman *mean*?' asked Charles Kingsley, and Cardinal Newman, who was one of the finest exponents of English prose, wasn't able to answer, or was he? I don't remember.)

And there were other points you raised – my uncertainty about 'that' and 'which' and, a much more serious blunder, my occasional confusion of 'who' and 'whom', the nominative for the accusative, and vice-versa. *Qui s'excuse, s'accuse.* Is 'Whom the gods love, die young' good grammar? 'Those whom the gods' etc., would be. I leave 'it' to you! But I agree with you that 'When Jock saw whom it was (i.e. Pauline) who was calling to bring the car up, after a late performance at the theatre in Bristol, he at once broke off his conversation with the other irritable waiting chauffeurs, especially when he saw that Alexey, who was standing beside her, and holding his umbrella over her, quite an effort for him, as he was shorter than she' ('she' is all right here, isn't it? for 'than' is wrongly used as a preposition, governing the *accusative* case) – this is all quite wrong, and unworthy of *Simonides on Ceos* which some people think my best book.

So many accusatives, so many accusations! I won't try to defend myself, except by saying that every now and then you seem to confuse the *pendent nominative* with the ablative absolute, which is admissible in English as it was in Latin. When Alexey says to Pauline, after her performance, not a very successful one, 'The rain having stopped, let us take a little stroll,' he was grammatically correct, if uncolloquial, being always something of a pedant (as well as a pendant!) And I suppose it was his pedantry that Pauline resented when she said, 'Oh no, let's go in now, I'm tired, and Jock will be waiting about, because we haven't given him his orders for tomorrow.' It was then that the little rift within the lute began – but you wouldn't know, you didn't read as far as that.

Well, a truce to the accusatives and accusations. If and when I write another novel, I shall ask you to vet it – you are such an expert fault-finder!

As for the book itself, what can I say? You don't like it, and that's all.

As Tennyson said of the Charge of the Light Brigade, – 'Theirs not to reason why.' Critics of such old standing as you must often say to yourselves, 'Oh, to hell with it! I don't *like* it!'

So let's scrub out your not liking 'it' (*The Love-Adept*, I mean). I am reminded of a passage in the book which you wouldn't have got up to, before you threw it aside. It is meant to illustrate another rift between the relationship of Pauline and Alexey – a rift which neither of them wanted. They were lunching together, and Alexey, after consulting Pauline, had ordered 'Chicken à la –', I can't remember what. When it came, Pauline took one bite of it, and pushed her plate away.

'I can't eat it,' she said. 'It's got garlic in it.'

'Don't you like garlic?' asked Alexey, anxiously beckoning to the waiter. 'I like it so much, just a taste, just a soupçon, and I believe it's good for you, too. Keeps off colds and so on. But I would never have ordered it if I had known you didn't like it.'

'I hate it,' said Pauline, 'dear Alexey, I absolutely hate it. And so does Jock. It gives him indigestion.'

'How do you know?' asked Alexey, rashly.

'I do know, my dear friend, isn't that enough?'

After a pause of twenty minutes or so, 'Chicken à la King was produced for Pauline.

'But you don't mind *me* eating something garlic-y?' asked Alexey. 'Two's company, three's none, if garlic makes the third.'

'With you, Alexey,' said Pauline, graciously, 'there can be no third.'

．　　　．　　　．

Well, you don't like garlic, either, do you, Elizabeth? Perhaps I was thinking of that when I wrote about Pauline and Alexey, *à deux* at luncheon.

But there is one thing I must tell you, and I know it will be a relief to you. *The Love-Adept* wasn't dedicated to you – it was meant for another Elizabeth. How different from each other people of the same name can be.

Yours, etc.,
James

James laid down his pen, and pondered. Was the letter too resentful, or not resentful enough? To turn the other cheek was Christian teaching; but surely one must react, one must answer back, or one becomes characterless, except as a doormat, a doormat for all the heavy-footed Elizabeths to tread on?

Elizabeth III was a friend of old-standing, and his letter might bring their friendship to an end. One cannot afford to lose friendships; but hadn't his been brought to an end by her? It was seven o'clock in the evening, an hour when for some unknown reason, James was at his most belligerent; in the morning, waking up with all his dismal thoughts about his past, his present and his future, he was as inoffensive as a sheep. Which of them was the true James? The caitiff of the early hours, with no come-back in him, or the swashbuckler of the evening, inspired by a few dry Martinis? He didn't know, but he knew how important it was to be himself, and just then his self, his reigning self, the self that counted, surely, by day and night, was utterly antagonistic to Elizabeth III. She meant something to him once, but now she was a bitch, just a bitch.

He rose from his desk and took the letter to the post-box.

'*Come along,*' *she said in a piercing whisper, '*it's* them!*'

Jean threw down her tea-towel and without waiting to hang it up to dry, planted herself in front of the looking-glass that flanked, and from some angles reflected, the kitchen-sink, that erstwhile centre of dramatic interest, thereby beating Fergus to it. Fergus wasn't interested in his appearance, but having been told he ought to straighten his tie he conscientiously tried to, diving this way and that under his sister's outstretched elbows, and sometimes standing on tiptoe to peer round her neck, for he knew that she, and Granny Kirkwood afterwards, might reprove him for not smartening himself up.

At last it was done, Jean's dress and Fergus's tie (being eight years old, he had only lately been promoted to wearing a tie).

'*Ready!*' *they cried in chorus, and stormed out of the kitchen. But on the threshold of the front room they halted. They were both daunted by the babble of voices within.*

'*You go first,*' *whispered Fergus.*

The top-light, seldom turned on, was quite blinding, and it took them a moment to take in the scene. All four were seated; Pauline and Alexey on the sofa facing them, Granny Kirkwood in the easy chair, and Jock their father, on a high chair opposite. He was the first to get up.

'*Hullo, children, how are you getting on?*'

*Almost in unison they replied, '*Very well, thank you, Dad.*'

Then there was an upsurge of adults. Kisses and embracements followed. Pauline knelt down and Alexey stooped down, as though by shortening their statures they could the better put themselves on the age-level of the children. Both Pauline, and Alexey, but especially Pauline, made a hubbub of almost inarticulate sounds such as people address to infants or to dogs. Jock stood aloof until their emotion had spent itself; then he bent down shyly and lifted first Jean and then Fergus to his lips. He put them down gently but slightly clumsily, and remained standing.

'But we must find somewhere for them to sit!' exclaimed Pauline. 'They mustn't stand, the little darlings!'

It was an awkward moment, for the chairs, like Musical Chairs, all seemed to have been bespoken.

'They can sit on the floor,' said Jock who was, after all, their father.

'Oh, no! How can you be so cruel, Jock!' And Pauline lifted her head brimming over with curls, towards them. 'Poor little angels, you must have had a tiring day.'

Jean didn't answer, but Fergus found his voice and said, 'Yes, Miss Pauline, but at school we have to sit all the time, or nearly all the time, except when we have to go out into the playground, so we don't a bit mind standing, do we, Jean?'

'I don't mind standing,' said Jean. 'I'm not sure if it's good for Fergus, because of his weak knee. He hurt it playing, Miss Pauline, boys are so rough.'

Fergus looked daggers at her, but Pauline said,

'It's all the more reason you should both sit down.' She turned to Alexey, who was sitting beside her on the sofa, and said,

'Alexey!'

'Yes, Pauline?'

'You sit on the arm of the sofa, and then Jean and Fergus, who don't take up any room at all, because angels don't take up any room – they can sit on the point of a needle, isn't that true? – Well, Jean and Fergus can sit on the sofa with me. Isn't that a good idea, Mrs. Kirkwood?'

'It's all according to how Mr. Alexey thinks,' said Mrs. Kirkwood, looking towards him, 'Mr. Alexey has to be considered, too.'

But Mr. Alexey was already on his feet. His straight fair hair, and his pinkish, unlined face, with the unshaded bulb beating down on it, made him look younger than he really was.

'Of course, Pauline; Jean and Fergus mustn't stand. I'll sit on the arm of the sofa, and they can sit beside you. There's plenty of room. And Jock –'

'Oh, I'm all right, sir,' Jock said, towering darkly behind them. 'I don't care whether I sit or stand.'

The word 'sir', suddenly dropping into this classless gathering, made ripples like a stone in a pool. But Pauline didn't seem to notice them.

'Come here, Jean, come here, Fergus.' She patted an invitation to them on the vacant places of the sofa. 'And you, Alexey, sit there!' She patted the left-hand shoulder of the sofa.

'And, as you, Jock, don't mind standing for a little bit' – she lifted her darkened eyelids towards him – 'well, let's talk about something. What shall we talk about?'

There was a silence, then Mrs. Kirkwood said tentatively,

'Well, Miss Pauline, I'm sure that the children and I would like to hear about your last trip. If Mr. Alexey knows about it already, I don't suppose he'll mind hearing about it again.'

Perched on the shoulder of the sofa, Alexey acknowledged this piece of tactfulness with a slightly downcast smile.

'As a matter of fact, Mrs. Kirkwood,' he said, using both hands to bestride his mount, instead of sitting side-saddle on it, 'I wasn't with Miss Pauline all the time – I joined her three – no – four days ago. So I'd be glad to hear of her experiences, and I dare say Jock knows something about them, too.'

'Oh, me?' said Jock, moving round a little so as to get their profiles as well as the backs of their heads into view, 'mine is just a log-book, so to speak – how we went, where we went, and, and . . . where we stayed. I don't think you'd be really interested in that,' he added quickly. 'I saw two or three of the shows, Miss Pauline kindly gave me tickets, and she came over fine, as she always does. She always gets a good hand and so many flowers – I don't know where she puts them!' – he added with a sudden smile. 'The lads are crazy about her, and some of the women, too.' He paused, wondering if he had said the right thing, and his dark eyes turned in their deep sockets, as if they were wondering, too. 'But one tour is very much like another, isn't it, Miss Pauline? Now Mr. Alexey, though he wasn't there all of the time, could tell you more about it than I could, because he was always in the front row, so to speak.'

He had put the ball into Alexey's court, and having said his say, he seemed to withdraw into his corner, his coign of vantage, or disadvantage, which his broad shoulders seemed to touch on either side, digesting his embarrassment. But I've said my piece anyhow, he thought, I've done what I could.

Alexey, thus appealed to, turned first to Jock, as if Jock had been the chairman, and then to the others, and said in a high and highly cultured voice, which contrasted strongly with Jock's strong Scottish accent, 'I don't think I have much to add to what Jock said. Without him and his know-how, in a score of ways, our little tour (I only came in at the tail-end of it), wouldn't have been half the fun it was. You've been kind enough to offer us each a glass of sherry; let's drink to you, Mrs. Kirkwood, and to Pauline, and to him.'

He looked round for his glass, which he had lost sight of when making way for Jean and Fergus, and seeing it on the table under the window, beneath the effigy of a large Alsatian dog, he reached for it, lifted it, and said, 'To us all'.

Mrs. Kirkwood, and Pauline, and Jock, who, by some sleight-of-hand, seemed to be ready with their glasses, raised them, too,

'To us all!'

'But what about Jean and Fergus?' said Pauline, in a deep semi-tragic voice. 'They haven't had anything, poor sweeties.'

'Oh, they've had their tea,' said Mrs. Kirkwood. 'We don't want to get them into bad ways, do we, Jock?'

'I didn't touch a drop of alcohol till I was fifteen,' said Jock, with a slightly virtuous air, eyeing the bottle of sherry and wondering whether its contents would go round a second time, if the children had their whack.

'But I've brought some chocolates for them,' said Pauline. 'Alexey and I have brought some chocolates for them, and some of the chocolates have liqueurs inside. You wouldn't mind that, would you, Mrs. Kirkwood? You are so kind.'

Jean and Fergus, who had hitherto maintained an uneasy silence, prompted by Mrs. Kirkwood's slight nudges and pursing of the lips, suddenly abandoned their non-co-operative attitude and exclaimed,

'Oh, yes!'

'Well, just this once.'

They looked on anxiously while Pauline fumbled in her bag. Supposing she had forgotten the chocolates? Grown-ups were as unpredictable as life was. At one moment a Mum, the next moment, none. Jock still seemed to be their Dad; but how long could they count on him remaining so, with Miss Pauline at his side? They couldn't count on anything, but yes, here were the chocolates.

There was much breaking of finger-nails while the box was being extracted from its packaging.

'Shall I try, Mr. Alexey?'

'Well, Jock, if you would be so kind.'

For the first time Jock advanced from his comfortable, or uncomfortable, standing-room in the corner, to the hub of their small universe. Under the pressure of his thick fingers, the chocolate-box soon gave up its secrets.

'Oh, Jock, how clever you are! What should we do without you?'

'It's nothing, Miss Pauline. You have to have strong finger-nails for that cellophane.'

'Well, you must have the first one, mustn't he, Alexey?'

'Of course, Pauline. Where should we be without Jock?'

'Stranded on some moor, I expect, some cellophane-girt moor, *with nowhere to go! No happy, comfortable domestic interior like this! Where are we actually going to, Alexey?'*

'To York, I think.'

'Do you agree, Jock?'

'Yes, Miss Pauline, you have an engagement there tomorrow night.'

'Goodness, I had almost forgotten. Thank you for reminding me. Alexey should have, but he's so scatter-brained.'

'Thank you, darling,' said Alexey, gratefully, 'but I did mention it.'

'I hate leaving here,' said Pauline, rising suddenly to her feet, 'I simply hate it. All these sweet people' (her glance embraced Mrs. Kirkwood and Jean and Fergus). 'I'm heart-broken to leave you, especially after all your kindness, and especially to go to York, York, of all places. Do you know anything about York, Jock?'

'Well, it's about fifty miles, and quite a fast road.'

'You don't know anything else about it?'

'Not much, Miss Pauline. Perhaps Mr. Alexey does.'

Alexey dismounted from his seat on the saddle of the sofa.

'What do you know about York, Alexey?' Pauline asked.

'Oh, well, it has a Minster.'

'Of course, you needn't tell me that.'

'And it has some city walls, and some Roman remains, and the ruins of a very beautiful Abbey, and some very fine Georgian houses, and a new University –'

'Oh, stop, stop. You make me want never to go there, and yet I must. Jock, is the car ready?'

'Yes, Miss Pauline. I've had it topped up.'

'I think I must powder my nose,' she said, making a gesture towards it. 'And I expect that you, Jock, would like to have a word with these little darlings, and with Mrs. Kirkwood who has been more, more than a mother to them. If we all had a Mrs. Kirkwood to look after us, how happy we should be . . . so kind, so very kind. . . .

Alexey, you will be comfortable in the car I hope.' She went to the door. 'It's this way, isn't it, Mrs. Kirkwood?'

'The first floor. I'll turn the light on. You can't miss it, but I'll show you.'

Jock was left with Jean and Fergus. He said, awkwardly,

'You're getting on O.K., are you? I wish I could see you oftener. Granny Kirkwood seems a good sort – I hope she looks after you all right.'

'Oh yes, Dad,' they said with one voice.

'I wish we had a home of our own,' he said. Coming near to them, and they coming near to him, he put his arms round their shoulders. 'Just now we can't, but perhaps we shall have later on. Miss Pauline is very good to me, and Mr. Alexey, he's not too bad, either. And they both like you, which is a good thing, even if Miss Pauline makes an act about it. Please remember that I don't forget you, either of you, though I never know where I shall be next, and you don't know where I shall be – but that follows, doesn't it? Miss Pauline is always running up and down the country, with Mr. Alexey sometimes alongside, sometimes not, it's a queer set-up, but I hope that before long we – you two and I – will be able to settle down together. Listen! There they are at the door. I must go. Be good to yourselves.'

He stooped and kissed them and before they could say good-bye he was gone.

CHAPTER IX

But why had Elizabeth IV not written? It was she he most
wanted to hear from, but not a word.

A languor descended on his spirits. That she, of all people,
should have failed to acknowledge his book! It was too bad, too
discouraging, too frustrating. Writing wasn't just a pastime,
not just work, not just a means (however precarious) of making
a living. It was a means of communication, not only with the
outside world, but more particularly, with one's friends.
James owed a great deal to the encouragement of his friends,
sometimes he thought he owed *everything*. And above all to
Elizabeth IV.

The other Elizabeths had all written to him, in their different
ways, about *The Love-Adept*, Elizabeth III not very kindly – let
us forget that. (So thought the early-morning James.)

But Elizabeth IV had not written, and as day followed day
James asked himself, 'Hasn't she received the book? Is it
becalmed in some post-office?' (The postal service was notori-
ously unreliable nowadays.) 'Or has she received it and is too
embarrassed to say what she thinks – or to make any comment
at all?'

The expedient of writing to her, to ask if the book had come
to hand, he dismissed. It would be ignominious for him, and
embarrassing for her. She might reply, as a hostess, well-known
in her day, had replied to him, when he sent her his lately-
published novel, 'I have been very fortunate this weekend.
No less than thirteen authors have sent me copies of their

books.' It wasn't likely that Elizabeth IV would have received so many. She moved in the literary world, but not in a promiscuous, undiscriminating way: and she was his special friend. If he had not persecuted her with his attentions, as Alexey had persecuted Pauline, he had rather pressed them on her (perhaps a feeling of guilt about this had been the germ of the novel). She had not discouraged him, nor had she encouraged him; but a feeling of satiety, where he was concerned, might well have been mounting in her, and *The Love-Adept*, with its demands on her limited reading-time, and her limited writing-time, might seem the last straw.

He pondered, as often before, on the sentence that Goethe put into the mouth of a character (a woman character) in *Wilhelm Meister*: 'The fact that I love you is no concern of yours.' Ideally, and regarded *sub specie aeternitatis*, this might be, and probably was, true: the fact that the wind blows on you, and the rain beats down on you, is no concern of yours, because it is the dictate of a higher Power, just as love is the dictate of a higher Power. But looked at practically and personally and *sub specie temporis* (would Elizabeth III pardon this expression? he doubted it) such a love as Alexey's for Pauline simply wasn't *on*. She wouldn't have tolerated it at all save for the material advantages it gave her – the Austin Princess, and the status symbol of being followed around whenever she appeared in public, by a well-to-do – and Alexey was well turned out as well as well-to-do – by a presentable if not very personable middle-aged man, a *cavaliere servente*, such as many women would have envied. And Jock, her uniformed chauffeur, with his good looks and his good manners which always made such an *éclatant* effect on hotel-receptionists, porters, hall-boys, theatre attendants, and so on – how could she afford his services without Alexey to foot the bill? If it is expensive to keep a woman, it is just as expensive to keep a hired car with chauffeur, etc.

These were the bare bones of the situation. James had tried to put some flesh on to them, and some heart into them. If only Elizabeth IV would write.

.   .   .

At last the letter came, and as so often happens, the explanation of its belatedness was as simple as it was unexpected. The stamp and the post-mark, St. Tropez, told him half and the rest was contained in her letter.

CHAPTER X

St. Tropez, A.M.
France

Dearest James,

How can I apologize enough for my long delay in thanking you for *The Love-Adept*? Somebody said, 'I apologize but I do not explain.' But I want to do both, and in more ways than one.

One part of the apology will be obvious, and I am sure you will feel it needs no defence. *The Love-Adept* came after I had left, and it had to be forwarded. Luckily for me, there was someone to forward it, but all that takes time. I was suddenly called away to the sick-bed of my dear aunt. She has always been an angel to me, and I went at a moment's notice, and hadn't time to tell anyone, even you, that I was going. There is very little I can do for her, the end of life is so sad, isn't it? Nothing to look forward to, nothing to hope for, nothing to *arrange* for – happily for her she has seen to all that. But at any rate I can be *with* her and whether she recognizes me, or whether she doesn't, makes little difference.

It is a solemn time, this waiting upon death, and somehow it takes the colour and even the *meaning* out of life. All the plans we make for ourselves, all the relationships, tempting or untempting, that we see ahead of us, what do they amount to? Nothing. The laughter of fools, thorns crackling under a pot.

I didn't mean to write to you in this gloomy strain, and I *could* have made it a subject for mirth – poor Aunt Jane, well over eighty, with several servants crowding round her, and solicitors, equally solicitous, and all piously hoping for her recovery, but all with an eye to their rake-off if she doesn't recover, as of course she won't.

But this is only part of my apology – the difficulty of assessing *life*, with its myriad possibilities, compared with the single fact of *death*. We have, at least I have, the illusion that we are immortal. We know we aren't, but unless we had the illusion, we should all live (if we could call it living) in the expectation, and under the threat of death. It wouldn't seem worthwhile to stir a finger to help or hinder us.

I only say this because the characters in *The Love-Adept* are to me (at any rate) so much alive. They live for money, no doubt: Alexey's wealth (no use to him, no emotional outlet, when he is by himself) becomes a dynamic source of happiness when he can share it with Pauline, and her boy-friend, Jock, his two children and their foster-mother, Mrs. Kirkwood. They are all looking forward to something, or perhaps dreading something, that life holds in store, and all of them too much engaged with life to be aware of the possibility of death. They aren't troubled by the thought of what might happen to them if Alexey had a heart-attack or a stroke; though they all are, even Pauline, self-confident as she is, troubled by the thought of what might happen if Alexey suddenly withdrew his favours.

I have read the book twice over – I found it compulsive reading – which is one of my excuses for not writing to you before. And I enjoyed it very much, dear James, and I can't thank you enough for telling me that I was the Elizabeth – the real, the only Elizabeth, you had meant the book for. You told me you didn't want to dedicate it to Elizabeth Prescott, in case I didn't like it, and then I could take refuge in the limbo of comparative anonymity with your other Elizabethan friends. But I shan't – oh no! I shall boast to the other Elizabeths (I expect I know one or two of them) that I am 'the onlie begetter' of the ensuing pages. They will go mad, of course, because each of them will think the book was meant for her, and you will find yourself in a worse jam than Pauline and Alexey and Jock, and Jean and Fergus, and Mrs. Kirkwood ultimately found themselves.

'Oh what a tangled web we weave,' dear James, 'when first we practise to deceive!' – for you must admit you were trying to deceive *someone* (some Elizabeth you like better than me, perhaps, but I hope not), when first you devised that 'open' dedication. 'Open' is a word sometimes applied to a cheque which the recipient is asked to fill in for the right amount; it saves time, and shows that one trusts him or *her*; but in case he or she, should turn out to be a crook, and steal all one's money, one puts 'Under ten guineas' or whatever sum one thinks will just cover the amount owed, at the top of the cheque, and initials it as a protection against such marauders, who daily increase.

But 'open' is not the *'mot juste'* in this context. Your intention was anything but 'open', and if you had written 'To Elizabeth (under ten guineas)', or whatever phrase, derived from the financial world, might be thought of as limiting the output, or the outgoing, of the affections, you would have been more honest, and given less cause for heart-burning.

'A sweeter woman n'er drew breath than my son's wife, Elizabeth.'

Who remembers Jean Ingelow now?

But I have always treasured that couplet as a tribute to all Elizabeths including my defeated rivals for *The Love-Adept* award.

I should be boasting about my success now, but there is no one here to boast to, except my poor Aunt who oddly enough, is called Elizabeth – what a *compelling* name it must be – and she can hardly understand *anything*, poor darling, and certainly not the honour you have conferred on me. For I do regard it as an honour.

As I said, I enjoyed *The Love-Adept* enormously, and I think you have succeeded wonderfully well in keeping the balance of relative importance between the members of the sextet. It isn't a trio – for Jean and Fergus and Mrs. Kirkwood keep droning away in the bass – in the basement, I was going to say, considering their lowly and subordinate position – but they are (in a sense) too vital to the story to be made the excuse for a poor pun.

I have some reservations, and I feel that as your dedicatee and beneficiary (or whatever is the opposite of benefactress) I ought to voice them. Have you noticed how often you use the word 'ought'? Perhaps I 'ought' not to voice them, but I think I will.

One of them sounds too ungrateful to our long friendship, which has meant so much to me, but I know you won't take it amiss, dear James. It has to do with the balance of sympathy – sympathy as opposed to proportion – for the characters in the book. I'm not contradicting myself: I think they all play their rightful parts as they might in a musical composition, but reading *The Love-Adept* superficially (though God forbid one should) one might conclude that Pauline, and Jock too, were just gold-diggers, battening on Alexey's bounty. But I think that is unfair. Being a man, you can't know how worrying it is for a woman (for the fair sex, I was going to say, but how old-fashioned it sounds!) to be *pestered* by a man's devotion, whether it be expressed in money, by daily letters, or (let us be frank) by his continual *presence*, spaniel-like, adoring. All the time, Pauline must have resented, and felt guilty for resenting, the fact that Alexey was giving her more than she was giving him. And Jock, hard-headed as he was, Arguseyed

97

to the main-chance – must have felt the same. It is one thing to hand out money, though I have never been in a position to do so, in order to satisfy some secret urge towards benefaction (you never said that Alexey and Pauline were lovers – he adored her from afar, and she would never, perhaps, have permitted a closer relationship) – but another thing to entertain the feelings of gratitude that such a recipient 'ought' to have. I could write you *reams* about gratitude, and I dare say you would understand them better than most people would. And it was the same with Jock: he was enjoying favours that he guessed were denied to Alexey (if they were), his employer and her protector; his children were being kept in comfort; but how could he feel as he 'ought' to feel, towards Alexey? He could be polite to him, as he always was, touching his cap and so on, when Alexey stumbled into view, partly because it ministered to his self-esteem (it was a good touch to make Alexey unsure on his feet – unsure of everything). I always liked that passage in the Bible when it suddenly says of Asa, 'However when he grew old, he was diseased in his feet.'

I said I had some reservations about the book, now I must tell you another, which is still more contradictory. (It is a woman's privilege to be illogical, isn't it?) But you don't really make enough, emotionally, of Alexey's obsession with Pauline. You tell us of the money he spent on her, and his determination, in season and out of season to be with her – but you make us sorrier for her than we are for him. I know you didn't mean her to be just the plaything of a well-off man. The letters he wrote to her every day, whether they were apart or together – his disappointment, his despair, when she didn't answer them – all these facts you make quite plain. He wanted to be all in all to her, but he couldn't be. Not because she didn't love him, not because she was in love with Jock, but because she couldn't *take* the weight, and volume and intensity of his affection. He piled it on her – without ever asking her (as far as I remember) if she loved him. She was ground down by it, she was suffocated by it. In all her thoughts, words and deeds he wanted to be present: it wasn't a rape on the body that he attempted – it was rape on the soul.

And the fact that she was a 'career-woman' made her position doubly difficult; she didn't want to keep him on but she couldn't without some considerable sacrifice of money and prestige, afford to let him go. If he went, it would mean that Jock also went, for she couldn't afford to keep him, either.

'Keep', what a word!

But somehow, in the end (but not quite in the end), it is the boredom of Pauline, being choked with cream in her gilded cage (forgive the mixed metaphor) that comes through most forcibly, and Jock's bewilderment, his uncertainty about what he 'ought' to do and what he 'ought' to feel, for he wasn't devoid of feeling, when the situation so suddenly and dramatically changes. I think that somehow you *could* have made Alexey's devotion seem deeper, in their triple relationship, than his purse and it would have strengthened the story.

That is why I particularly enjoyed the chapters where you show the relationship beginning to break up, and make us, or me, feel that Alexey's stake in it was greater than we (or I) had imagined.

Do read them again. To me, they are the highlight of the book and I have read them several times.

But the actual ending still puzzles me. Of course I know what *happened*, but what exactly do you intend by it? Is it meant to be cynical, as so much of the story is, or just *natural* and inevitable?

At the end you suddenly seem to change your mind about it all. I wonder why? The volte-face has the virtue of surprise, of course, but it didn't make sense to me.

Do write and tell me – I shall be here as long as my aunt is here. I can't say how long that will be. And don't think I am staying here for any other motive than that of *pure affection*. I am *not* like some of the characters in your book, whose 'motivation' is so suspect. I am always and most gratefully

Yours, Elizabeth ? ? ? ?

Elizabeth Prescott

P.S. How hard it is to reconcile the reality of fiction, for it has its own reality, with the reality of death! If I had been reading your book with an untroubled mind, with nothing to distract me from the printed page, I might have felt your imaginings more deeply than I have.

CHAPTER XI

James laid down Elizabeth Prescott's letter, and performed the small act of gratitude – without words, without genu-flexions – that he always registered on the receipt of any mercy, great or small. It wasn't superstitious, it was just an acknow-ledgement. He felt that Someone should be thanked.

Then he began (how Elizabeth III would have disliked this locution) to analyse his sensations. Relief was uppermost; Elizabeth IV had liked the book, and given valid reasons for not saying so before. His author's vanity was appeased and gratified; she hadn't looked his gift-horse in the mouth. All unknown to himself, he had intruded on her private grief. Art is long, and time is fleeting, but while time lasts, it has the upper hand. He felt as if he had been dancing on a grave-stone – an error of taste, to say the least. But he couldn't have known it; he couldn't have known that this fiction of his imagination, much as it meant to him, would be read by the eyes of someone to whom the reality of death was far more important than saying 'yes' or 'no' to a novel.

He tried to think that this explained her 'reservations'. 'Don't talk to me now, because I can't listen to you.' All the same, the 'reservations' chafed him; they were like the pea under a hundred feather-beds that irked the Real Princess. He was like a gardener who dislikes weeds more than he likes flowers.

Pauline was bored by Alexey's inordinate affection; and at the same time he (James) hadn't made the true value of Alexey's devotion to her apparent.

As human beings, entrusted with each other's happiness, she had devalued them both. To her, Elizabeth IV, in their different ways they were light-weight, playing at life instead of living it. Her death-bed vigil may have encouraged this conviction: it was no time for novel-reading.

But James had meant his *dramatis personae* to be representative human beings: not more superficial than their fellows, but certainly not less, and counting for as much, or as little, should death overtake them, as they had in life.

Perhaps he hadn't been able to distinguish between infatuation and love: but how difficult they were to distinguish! He had himself at one time thought himself in love with Elizabeth Prescott: hence the dedication. Had she found his attentions irksome to the serious purpose of the career-girl that she had been, or to the career-woman that she still was? Had his ardour lacked the stuff that dreams are made of?

But all this speculation was beside the point. She had asked him to comment on, to 'explain' the book's conclusion, and much as he disliked re-reading his own work it might be a help if he turned to the chapters where everything was in the melting-pot.

'Do you mind if Jock lunches with us, Alexey?'

'Of course not. He has often lunched with us, Pauline.'

'Yes, but I have thought, just lately, that you didn't want him to. Only an idea of mine, perhaps.'

'It certainly was. I like Jock very much. How could we get on without him?'

'Oh, I don't know. He can be difficult at times. I see more of him than you do.'

'Yes, Pauline?'

'You needn't say "yes" in that funny way, as if I was concealing something from you, because I'm not, I'm trying to tell you something.'

'What are you trying to tell me?'

'Please don't be sarcastic, or I can't tell you.'

'I didn't mean to be sarcastic. Please tell me.'

'Well, Jock has been running around just lately.'

'Running around?'

'Oh, Alexey, don't be stupid. I mean he has been neglecting us a bit, in favour of other things, other attractions, if you know what I mean. He's not so attentive as he used to be.'

'I hadn't noticed it, Pauline.'

'No, because your head is in the clouds.'

'But if it is, I can always see you. I can see you just as well, or better, in the clouds.'

'Nonsense, nonsense. Well, yes, all right. But Jock isn't a cloud-dweller. He has his foot firmly fixed on the accelerator. He doesn't care a damn for us. That's what I meant.'

'Oh Pauline, you must be imagining things. I don't know anything about Jock's private life, how should I? – except that he seems to like us, and he's devoted to his two children.'

'Yes, and that's partly why he seems to like us, because we help him to look after his children – or you do, Alexey, let's face it. But supposing he has another interest on the side –'

'He may have, but how does that affect you and me?'

'Oh not at all, not at all, except that I thought you'd rather know. As a matter of fact I thought you did know, as you've been a bit dry with him just lately.'

'Dry, Pauline?'

'It's a working-class expression that you wouldn't understand. I come from working-class people myself – that's how I know. It means short, curt, slightly snubbing, if you see what I mean. Dry as opposed to –'

'Wet?' suggested Alexey.

Pauline laughed.

'Well, you said it, I didn't. You are wet sometimes, but it's worse to be wet through! No, I thought you were a bit abrupt with him that day, when was it, Wednesday? – when he turned up late, and ran it rather fine getting to the Excelsior in time.'

They were sitting in the lounge of their hotel, waiting for their morning aperitifs. Alexey looked up at Pauline; he would have had to look up at her, for she was taller than he was, even if he hadn't been sitting in a lower chair.

He knit his brows, which were strangely unlined for his age, over his pale blue eyes, and looked into her dark eyes.

'Yes, Pauline, I do remember, but I thought it was you who were rather "dry" with him. You had every reason to be. You have to be before time – I only have to be in time.'

'That's true, Alexey. But you're sure you weren't annoyed with him for letting me down? Think how awful if they'd had to hold the curtain!'

'It certainly would have been,' said Alexey warmly, 'but thank goodness it wasn't. You may have been a bit rushed, but still you made it.'

'Thank goodness, but not Jock's goodness,' rejoined Pauline. 'Really, I think you should take a firmer line with him. After all, he's only a paid driver – it's his duty to consider us, not to beetle off on his own, or any one else's, if you see what I mean.'

'I didn't think you wanted me to take a firm line with him, Pauline.'

'Perhaps not, perhaps not, at the beginning. But if you give these people an inch, they take an ell. I know, because I was brought up with them. I know their tricks and their manners, as the doll's dressmaker said.'

'How well you know your Dickens!' said Alexey, genuinely admiring. 'But I think you're a little hard on Jock. He's never been late before. I expect he was just having another pint at the local.'

'Another pint at the local! Well, that's one way of putting it. But even if he had been, he shouldn't take a drink before he drives. Breathalysers and all that.'

A waiter in a white coat appeared threading his way across the sumptuous lounge, bringing Pauline her habitual Dubonnet, and Alexey his habitual dry martini. He bowed to them both, with a slight difference of deference to each, to Pauline, because she was almost a celebrity, and to Alexey, because he paid.

They drank together, and separately, in silence. The drink loosened Alexey's tongue.

'Jock will be here any time now.'

'Do you really not want him to lunch with us, Alexey? These four-star hotels always give meals to chauffeurs, at quite a small cost, I believe. And they are happier,' she added, raising her eyebrows and looking down at him, 'eating with their own kind.'

'Eating with their own kind?' asked Alexey, who hadn't quite caught on, 'or eating their own kind?'

Pauline gave a rich throaty laugh.

'Both, I dare say.'

Alexey sipped his drink.

'Do you still not want Jock to lunch with us?'

'I, my dear Alexey? I don't understand. I thought it was you who didn't want him to lunch with us. Class distinctions, and all that. You have always been tolerant about them, but you must remember that people of Jock's sort (mind you, he's a good fellow, as they go), they take advantage if they get the chance.'

'I'm afraid we must have him today,' said Alexey, in a lowered voice. 'We invited him, didn't we, at least, you did. And I see him coming – it would be too unkind if we asked him to go away to the chauffeurs' room, if there is one.'

.   .   .

'What will you have to drink, Jock?'

'A small Teacher's, Mr. Alexey, thank you.'

' "Teacher's"?'

'Oh, any sort of whisky.'

'But wouldn't you rather have a large one? A large teacher is better than a small teacher, at least that was my experience at school.'

Jock tried to catch Pauline's eye, not quite successfully (how frustrating and embarrassing is a wink unreturned) and laughed.

'I don't go much on drink,' he said, 'but I do like a Scotch now and then, and they say Teacher's is the best, its mellower, somehow.'

He was ill at ease, obviously pining for the drink to come. 'For the drink to come.' How fiercely Elizabeth III would have pounced on this ambiguity. (Somehow James couldn't get her out of his mind.) Meanwhile he watched Jock crossing and re-crossing his long, navy-blue-clad legs, until finally he adopted an attitude which was obviously easier for him – both legs well apart, and a large hand clutching each knee.

'Don't be impatient, Jock,' Pauline said. 'He'll be here in a minute or two.'

Jock's face registered a hit, and Alexey, to cover his confusion, said, 'He's on his way now.'

Jock took a good swig and looked happier.

'Sorry I was late,' he said, 'trouble with the car, you know. It's the magneto this time – never a dull moment, is there?'

Sitting on Pauline's left, he looked anxiously at both of them, hoping that his well-worn witticism had gone down well. 'But it's all right now, Miss Pauline, or perhaps I should say, Mr. Alexey sir.' He often addressed them by this dual title.

There was a slight pause, and then Pauline said in her slightly actressy voice.

'What is all right, now, Jock?'

'The car, Miss Pauline.'

'Oh, the car.'

Her tone suggested that it didn't matter much whether the car was all right or all wrong.

'But we haven't ordered yet,' she went on scanning the menu. 'Smoked salmon for us – I know you like it, Alexey, and for you, Jock?'

Jock cast troubled eyes down the mostly French-written bill-of-fare. Recognizing a word he knew, he said.

'Chump chop, please, Miss Pauline.'

'Chump chop?' she repeated, with the unconscious instinct of an actress mimicking his voice. 'Chump chop. But nothing to begin with? No smoked salmon?'

'No thank you, Miss Pauline. Perhaps a little soup.'

'Perhaps a little soup! Thick or clear?'

'Thick, please, Miss Pauline.'

'I think I'll change my mind,' said Alexey, suddenly. 'I'll follow Jock, and have some thick soup, too.'

'But I thought you never ate soup at luncheon, Alexey?'

'*Well, eat it or drink it, I think to-day I will.*'

Jock gave him a grateful look. Pauline sighed and shrugged her shoulders.

'*And will you join Jock in the chump chop?*'

'*I wish I could, Pauline. But my teeth, or my lack of teeth, won't stand up to it. May I look at the menu?*'

With a slightly injured air Pauline handed it to him.

'*But of course, my dear boy. How thoughtless of me – but not really thoughtless, because generally we like the same things – to eat, at any rate.*'

Alexey took the bill of fare, and turned it towards Pauline.

'*But you haven't chosen anything yet.*'

'*Oh no,*' *she said, casting her eyes down on the reddish, foreign handwriting,* '*I haven't. But of course I don't count,*' *and she laughed at herself.* '*I think I'll have some ris de veau, sweetbreads aren't they? Some people don't like innards, but I find them very digestible.*'

'*I'll join you,*' *Alexey said.*

'*Peas, carrots, beans, potatoes, cauliflower or tomatoes?*' *rattled off the waiter, bending over them, pencil poised.*

'*Oh just peas for me.*'

'*And for me too,*' *said Alexey.* '*And what will you have, Jock?*'

'*It's my day out. I think I'll have the lot,*' *Jock said.*

They laughed, with him and at him.

'*And wine? A carafe of white wine, what do you think, Pauline?*'

'*Perfect.*'

'*And for you, Jock?*'

'*Another drop of Scotch, Mr. Alexey, please.*'

For a time all went well. They conversed, and Jock, munching his chop, with his knife and fork spread facing each way on his plate, and his elbows turned outwards, to correspond, and his face turned downwards, did what he could to help the conversation. Every now and then he tried to catch Pauline's eye, but she seemed to avoid his, whereas Alexey met his glance as of yore.

'What's up?' Jock asked himself, 'what's up? Has she found a bloke she likes better than me? In the mirror on the wall opposite he studied his reflection; his hair might be going back a bit, as any man's might at the age of thirty-five, but otherwise he was hale and hearty, and quite a match for any man in the room. He regretted that he had had the shoulders of his 'good' suit padded, they didn't need it; and the sleeves were a trifle short; they left too much white shirt-cuff showing above his thick wrists. He pulled them down when no one seemed to be looking, and said,

'What orders, Miss Pauline, for the afternoon?'

'The afternoon?' repeated Pauline, vaguely. She looked at her jewelled watch, a present from Alexey. 'Oh yes, I suppose it is the afternoon. Shall we go somewhere, Alexey, shall we do a little sight-seeing?'

'Whatever you think, Pauline.'

'We might look at some of those abbeys, Yorkshire is full of abbeys, so I'm told.'

'Yes, there are some very nice abbeys in Yorkshire, Miss Pauline,' put in Jock, feeling that he must contribute to the conversation.

'Nice abbeys, Jock?' repeated Pauline, in a voice well-balanced between sarcasm and surprise. 'Are abbeys exactly nice?'

'Well, Miss Pauline, some very good abbeys. As you know, they were very religious in Yorkshire in times past, long before the days of motor-cars or anything like that. Of course they hadn't much to do except build abbeys, in those days, not much help for the working-man, I mean. They were just varlets, whatever that means.'

'I'm sure you are right,' said Pauline in a tragic tone. 'I'm sure you are right – the Scotch are so well-educated.'

'Excuse me,' said Alexey, trying to put his oar in, 'excuse me, Jock. You drive about the country a lot, and see places; but how did you know there were so many abbeys in Yorkshire?'

'I expect I read it in a book,' said Jock, 'or perhaps it was just taking people to see them. People go mad about abbeys, especially

Americans – Whitby Abbey, Bylands Abbey, Rievaulx Abbey, Kirkstall Abbey – that's very convenient for Leeds – Bolton Abbey, oh, it's a real beauty, you ought to see it, Mr. Alexey, and you too, Miss Pauline.'

Bored with this recital Pauline raised her eyes from the table and began to look round the room. Some of the other lunchers also raised their eyes and, recognizing the beautiful woman who had several times appeared on television, gave each other meaning looks and even nudged each other. Jock, with his stature and his beautiful head, also came in for comment; only Alexey was ignored.

But Jock, for reasons of his own, as it turned out, couldn't leave the subject of abbeys. In the bar he knew quite well what to say, and if anyone didn't like it he was prepared to go outside, and defend himself with his fists. Here he was at a loss; he couldn't summon Miss Pauline or Mr. Alexey outside and thump them, even if he had wanted to. It would have been very bad policy.

All the same, he wanted to say his say, and keep his end up in the conversation.

'There are all sorts of lovely abbeys,' he went on, leaning forward and offering them the contents of his cigarette-case, a gift from Alexey. When they both refused, he asked 'May I smoke?' and when they had given him leave, he proceeded:

'All sorts of lovely abbeys, because of course, they were so religious in those days.'

'Are you religious?' asked Pauline, negligently, as if it didn't matter if he was.

'Oh no, Miss Pauline,' said Jock, shocked, 'I'm a Presbyterian.'

Here Alexey felt he 'ought' to intervene.

'It doesn't follow,' he said, rather pompously, 'that because you are a Presbyterian, Jock, therefore you are not religious. A great many, indeed most, Presbyterians are religious – John Knox, for instance.' He gave Jock a look, who lowered his blue-black eyes. Touché.

'Religion isn't a matter of creed,' pronounced Alexey, 'is it, Pauline?'

Pauline felt for her bag beside her chair.

'Darling,' she said, 'I wouldn't know.'

Alexey lifted his hand, and his eyebrows, to attract the head-waiter, or any waiter, to bring him the bill.

'No, it isn't,' he went on, finishing his glass. 'It's a state of mind, a state of the heart, a state of the soul.'

'Oh, darling,' said Pauline, studying her face, and adding a touch, here and there. 'How serious you are.'

'I'm not being serious,' retorted Alexey, with half an eye on the bill which the waiter, hovering above them, wreathed in smiles, had just brought. Was the service-charge included in that muddle of figures at the foot of the bill? Footing the bill! It wasn't good manners to look. He gave some notes to the waiter, and went on:

'I'm not being serious, in the bad sense. I was trying to persuade Jock that Presbyterianism and religion weren't incompatible.'

Jock grinned.

'It's a question of how you behave, Mr. Alexey, sir, isn't it? Now some people –'

'We won't go into that,' said Alexey, unusually firm, 'we won't go into that. Let's go and see this abbey, wherever it is.'

'It's quite near, quite near my home,' said Jock. He hesitated. 'I mean, quite near the house of Mrs. Kirkwood who has been kind enough to look after my children during the . . . during the temporary absence of their mother, I mean, my wife. You know it, Miss Pauline, because you've been there before, and so have you, Mr. Alexey, sir. It's only a small place, you mightn't have noticed it.' Embarrassed, he glanced from one to the other. 'Perhaps I shall have a place of my own sometime. This is just lodgings, if you know what I mean . . .' His voice trailed away, and then he added, more hopefully, 'But this abbey, it's only a mile or two away, a really good abbey, visitors come to it in shoals, and I think it's only one and sixpence entrance –

I'm not sure about the sixpence. I could have a word or two with the kids, while you are looking at the ruins, and then I could pick you up at any time you say. I'm sure Mrs. Kirkwood would be glad to give you a cup of tea – she did once before, if you remember.'

'What shall we do, Alexey?' asked Pauline, rising. 'What shall we do?' she repeated almost tragically. 'Shall we go and look at this abbey?'

She pronounced the word as if it was an imprecation. Sometimes she fell into this tragedy-queen way of speaking: it was a relic of old days, when, as a budding actress, she had to study Shakespearian rôles. And she was a natural mimic: if they amused her, or if she wanted to make an impression, she could hardly help imitating the facial expression, the gestures and the voice and accent, of her latest interlocutor. Alexey relished these impersonations very much, as she well knew.

'All right, let's go and see the abbey,' he said. 'What is it called, Jock?'

'It's called Wharfedale Abbey – Miss Pauline, Mr. Alexey, sir. It's a really fine abbey. All the guide-books recommend it. It's a Cistercian abbey – not like some of those other abbeys.'

'Goodness, Jock, what a lot you know!'

'I have to, Mr. Alexey, seeing as I drive people about in the way I do, it's part of my job, they want to know what they're looking at, and you can't blame them. There were Benedictine abbeys, they were the first, and then there were Cistercian abbeys, and then there were Augustinian abbeys.'

'I'm not sure you are right there, Jock,' interrupted Alexey. 'The Augustinians built priories – they were secular canons, in a manner of speaking. Beverley Minster was an Augustinian foundation.'

'No doubt you're right, sir,' said Jock, with a hasty glance at Pauline whose eyes were closing. 'But Beverley Minster is a long way away. Yorkshire is the broad-acred shire.'

'Broad-acred what?' asked Pauline, surfacing.

'Shire, Miss Pauline. The distances are long, but I could take you to Beverley, only we should have to top up the car with petrol.'

'For God's sake, no,' said Pauline assembling her impedimenta. 'One abbey is quite enough for one day, don't you think so, Alexey?'

Alexey agreed, and they set off.

Wharfedale Abbey, as its name implies, is situated in Wharfedale, on the banks of the Wharfe. Its position is not so breathtakingly beautiful as the abbeys of Bolton and Tintern and Rievaulx, nor do its ruins vie in architectural interest with those of Fountains, or Much Wenlock or Crowland. But all the same, Jock was right to call it a 'fine' abbey.

'Shall I wait for you, Miss Pauline, Mr. Alexey, sir?' he asked. 'I can 'phone from a call-box near here if those so and so's haven't wrecked it, and it would be quicker than going back to my own place, and save petrol too.'

'Shall we ask him to wait, Alexey?'

'Oh, I think so, don't you, Pauline? It won't take us long to have a look at the ruins. The choir is the best part, so the guide-book says. A very fine example of Early English. I like to try to reconstruct in my mind what the finished building would have looked like, don't you?'

'I like anything that you like, Alexey.'

Jock was still hovering in the background.

'Well, let's ask Jock to stay. And then, if he wants to go home –'

'Home, Alexey?'

'If he wants to go and see his children –'

'I'm sure Mrs. Kirkwood would be glad to give you a cup of tea,' said Jock, 'I'll go and ring her up.' And before they had time to change their minds – or Pauline's mind – he was off.

.   .   .

'We're in the middle of the building now,' said Alexey, almost excitedly. 'The nave, or what's left of it, is behind us, on our left

114

was the north transept. And above us would have been the central tower. That's correct, isn't it?' he said, appealing to the guide.

'Quite correct, sir.'

'What a pity that so many central towers fell down. A church, a church of this size – I don't mean a parish church – is incomplete without a central tower. If only Westminster Abbey had had a central tower, or if Winchester Cathedral had something taller than that stumpy little hat-box! Think of the glorious central towers of Lincoln, and Canterbury, and Durham, and Gloucester!'

'Yes, indeed,' said Pauline, but Alexey was too much engrossed with his vision of central towers to notice that she wasn't thinking of them.

'Every cathedral, every life, for we are all cathedrals of a sort, however puny, and built in different styles, at different dates, needs a central tower, to pull it together, architecturally, I mean. You are mine, Pauline.'

Once Pauline realized the personal drift of Alexey's remarks, she caught on at once.

'And you are mine, Alexey!'

They turned towards each other, and gazed upwards into the empty space of darkening sky where the central tower should have been.

The guide looked at them with sympathy but without surprise: he had seen so many tourists holding hands.

Giving them time to recollect themselves, he said, turning eastwards:

'Now, this is the choir, built by Abbot Jocelyn in 1260. A very fine example of the Early English style. It's a pity that only the arches of the pier-arcade – I mean those big arches on the ground floor – are left, and just some bits of the triforium.' He waved towards them, 'And the East window – it was Decorated of course, as you would know, sir – for you can still see some fragments of the tracery. It's a shame that these fine old buildings had to be pulled *down, or let fall down, but it was all to do with religion, as you know, sir. The Disillusion of the Monasteries, such a mistake, but of course it gives people like me a living.'*

As they were turning away, Alexey asked him:

'Do you know when the central tower fell down?'

'It fell down twice, sir, but I couldn't tell you exactly when.'

.   .   .

Having finished their tour and suitably thanked their guide, Pauline and Alexey returned to the Austin Princess.

Jock was dozing, his head pillowed on the wheel.

'Not very attentive, is he?' said Pauline. 'A chauffeur ought to jump to it.'

'Oh, I expect he's tired,' said Alexey, and at that moment Jock opened his eyes and did jump to it.

'Would you like to come back to my place, Miss Pauline, sir, Mr. Alexey?' Confused by his nap, he didn't get the genders of his employers right. 'I phoned Mrs. Kirkwood, and she said she would be very pleased if you would come. And I shall see the kids, too,' he added.

'What do you say, Alexey?' asked Pauline, drawing her fur coat round her, with a slight shiver, whether for the cool evening breeze, or for the prospect of tea at Jock's place, or both, Alexey couldn't tell. 'Shall we go?' she added, as if a great deal depended on it.

'Oh yes, I think so,' said Alexey.

'I should like a cup of tea, after all this sight-seeing, and it would be nice to see Jock's children, wouldn't it? Children add so much to life.'

'Oh, do they?' asked Pauline, a little sceptically, 'sometimes they take away from it. But yes, I suppose they do. And Mrs. Kirkwood, we mustn't forget her, must we, Jock, such a dear woman.'

'Right-oh, Jock,' said Alexey, 'you know the way.'

There were lights in the front room, as of course there would be, when Mrs. Kirkwood was expecting company. February is a dark month, especially in Yorkshire.

'I'll get out and tell them you are here,' Jock said and began to disengage himself from the car, [why not just 'disengaged himself', James?] with much alacrity for so big a man. They watched him walking with long eager strides towards the house. As soon as the door was opened, he stood, cap in hand, silhouetted against the glow coming from the doorway, which he seemed almost to fill. They expected him to come back at any moment, but he did not come.

'Not very good manners is it,' said Pauline, 'to keep us waiting so long?'

'I expect the children are making a fuss of him,' said Alexey. 'Poor motherless little brats.'

At last Jock reappeared, walking towards them, slowly and reluctantly. His back to such light as there was, they could not read his expression [oh that pendent nominative! Apologies, Elizabeth III].

Opening the car-door on Pauline's side he said, 'I'm sorry to have to tell you, Miss Pauline, but there's been a bit of an upset in there.'

'Oh, what?' asked Pauline, interested at once.

Jock scratched his head where the hair was 'beginning' to grow thin, and said with a lapse into the vernacular very different from the correct diction on which he prided himself, 'I don't know that I can rightly tell you.'

'Oh come on, tell us!' cried Pauline. 'Has there been a murder?'

'Oh no,' said Jock, slightly relieved but still apprehensive. 'Just . . . just an unexpected guest, and uninvited too.'

'Man or woman?'

'Well, woman, as a matter of fact.'

'Oh, but we must see her! Why are you so cagey about her, Jock?'

Jock shuffled on his feet, obviously embarrassed, and clasped the handle of the door as if for support.

'I don't think she's the type who would interest you or Mr. Alexey,' he said at last.

'But I'm sure she would! I meet all sorts of types going up and down the country, I do, and so does Mr. Alexey, don't you, Alexey?' He murmured assent.

'What snobs you must think us, Jock! I didn't know you had such a bad opinion of us.'

'It isn't altogether that,' said Jock, 'it isn't altogether that. It's because . . .', words failed him.

'Oh, nonsense,' said Pauline, 'I believe it's just some skeleton in the cupboard that you're hiding from us! What do you think, Alexey?'

'I think we should respect Jock's wishes, dearest.' 'Dearest' was a sign of his agitation, for he knew she didn't like him to call her 'dearest' in public, or in private, for that matter. She might be dearest to him, but he wasn't dearest to her, not by a long chalk. Jock had been much, much dearer, until— The word 'dearest' not only irritated her, it made her feel guilty because she couldn't return the affection it implied.

'Well, you stay behind if you like,' she said, 'I'm going anyhow, and I think it's rather bad manners not to go, when Mrs. Kirkwood is expecting us. I'm getting out! Come on, Alexey!' and she pushed at the door, so that Jock, however unwilling he was, had to open it for her. Alexey dismounted from the other side.

'I'll go ahead,' said Jock, as if he was announcing a death, and like [like? like?] a funeral cortège they proceeded towards the closed door of the house.

Once inside they found Mrs. Kirkwood wearing the bright but slightly strained smile of welcome that many hostesses have to assume. Jean and Fergus came forward politely to shake hands with their father and Mr. Alexey and Miss Pauline, but they were obviously more interested in the glamorous stranger already in their midst. Not quite a stranger, perhaps, although they hardly remembered their mother after all these years, but glamorous certainly: very pretty, much made up, and only just on the wrong side of thirty.

'Miss Pauline, Mr. Alexey, sir,' began Jock, passing the buck to Mrs. Kirkwood, 'will you introduce us, please?'

'Of course, Jock,' she said coming to the rescue, as she thought, 'this is Miss Pauline, this is Mr. Alexey (we all call each other by our first names), and this is' – she hesitated a moment – 'this is Gina.'

Pauline swam towards her.

'Delighted to meet such a beautiful girl. You would make a fortune on the movies, Gina.'

Gina did not take Pauline's outstretched hand. She backed away, with a hostile gleam from her half-closed eyes.

Jock interposed his bulk between them, eclipsing them from each other.

Pauline dropped her hand to her side.

'Why, what's the matter with her?' she asked. 'Does she think I've got the plague, or something? I only made a civil remark.'

'She's like that sometimes,' said Jock, giving Pauline a quick backward look. 'She's funny, sometimes. Don't pay any attention, Miss Pauline.' He continued to stand between them, intercepting them, like the 'He' in Blind Man's Buff. 'But I think we'd better go away now, Miss Pauline and Mr. Alexey, sir, in case she spoils the party.'

Pauline, screened by Jock's broad shoulders, couldn't see much of what was going on in the small, over-furnished, brightly lit room, but she caught the eye of Mrs. Kirkwood, who was talking to Alexey and the children, in a corner half-right from her.

'I don't see why we should go away just because she's rude, do you, Mrs. Kirkwood? After all, you're our hostess, it's your house, and you asked us to come. From what Jock told me, you didn't ask her.'

'She didn't ask me,' spluttered Gina, 'and shall I tell you why? Because Jock told her not to – that's why.'

'Would anyone like another cup of tea?' asked Mrs. Kirkwood, advancing pacifically with the tea-pot. 'There's plenty more where this comes from, and it would be a shame to waste it.' She brandished it invitingly, with a circular motion that included everyone. 'A good cup of tea makes such a difference, don't you think? Now you, Miss Pauline,' she said, edging behind Jock's back, 'you've hardly tasted yours. Would you like some more milk or sugar? Or would you like a fresh cup? I can easily get one.'

'I'm afraid I couldn't touch it,' said Pauline. 'I've never been so insulted in my life. That woman! If Jock was the man he seems to be –.'

'That woman!' exploded Gina, still invisible to Pauline behind Jock's ample frame. 'That woman, I like that. And what do you think you are, Miss Pauline? You're a kept woman, kept by that man in the corner there, I don't know what his name is, but it isn't English, and you're serviced by Jock, in more ways than one!'

Mrs. Kirkwood put the tea-pot down on its tray. Alexey was still talking to Jean and Fergus, in the persuasive and encouraging tones of someone organizing a children's party.

Gina went on, 'You didn't think I knew all about this, did you? But when Jock was driving me in that posh car –'

'Oh it was you he was driving in our car, was it?' said Pauline. 'I saw you, you hollow-faced strumpet! And you, Jock, what right had you to use our car and our petrol to drive this old so-and-so around?'

Jock tried to keep his head.

'I've drove her once or twice, Miss Pauline and Mr. Alexey, sir,' he said. 'You told me I could use the car, if I wanted to, when you did not require it. And I always paid for the petrol.'

'And you wanted to drive this woman?' cried Pauline, at last dodging round Jock's shoulder so as to get a full view of her enemy. 'This bitch!'

'Bitch? Now I'll tell you something,' said Gina, advancing slowly on Pauline. 'I'm not a bitch, even if you are. I'm Jock's wedded wife, and I've come to claim him, and the children too. That's why I'm here, to take him back!'

'Wedded wife?' said Pauline, her histrionic ability coming to her aid. 'Wedded wife, indeed! Unwedded mistress of a nigger, from what I've heard! And yet you have the sauce, you cheeky monkey, to come back here –'

Gina made a dive at her, which was foiled by Jock's left arm. His right hand came across and hit Gina in the mouth. She dropped to the floor, bleeding and moaning. There was no other sound in the room, except the gusty crying of the children.

Alexey stood in front of them, executing an impromptu dance most unsuitable to his age, flapping his arms like the sails of a windmill to shield them from what they saw, or might see, and uttering inarticulate but reassuring sounds.

Gina was still lying on the floor and her blood began [yes, began, Elizabeth III] to stain the carpet, Mrs. Kirkwood's new carpet.

'I'll put a tea-towel under her head,' said Mrs. Kirkwood. She went into the kitchen and returned with a gaily-coloured cloth, that matched Gina's red dress, and her blood. 'And you, Jock, go and ring up the police while I'm wiping her mouth. Only I haven't a clean handkerchief.'

'Here's one,' said Alexey, offering an immaculate square of cambric from his breast-pocket. He looked round.

'But oughtn't we to give her something?'

'Give her something?' said Jock, 'a kick in the pants, perhaps. But why ring up the police? She's only shamming. An ambulance, if you like. I'd take her to the hospital myself, only I don't want to muck up Mr. Alexey's car.'

Mrs. Kirkwood disregarded him.

'Thank you, Mr. Alexey,' she said. 'I'll dial 999, and then I'll wash this out.' She held the handkerchief between the tips of her fingers. 'I won't be messed about any more,' she said, suddenly angry. 'Excuse me, ladies and gentlemen, but the 'phone is in the kitchen.'

Her departure made a sort of détente. Jean and Fergus stopped crying; Alexey gave up his windmill flailings, and they all converged round the prostrate form of Gina, who opened her eyes now and then.

'Don't worry about the car, Jock,' whispered Alexey. 'Just take her to the nearest hospital, if you know which it is. It would be much the best way.'

'I wouldn't like to move her,' said Jock, going back on what he had

previously said. 'You shouldn't move them, if they have had a fall.'
He spoke generally, not connecting himself with Gina's fall.

But Mrs. Kirkwood was by now on the telephone, and they could hear through the wall the whirring sounds thrice repeated. They pierced the silence of the sitting-room as if they had been the start-and-stop whinings of a circular saw. But what she said, or what the answer was, could not be heard.

Mrs. Kirkwood didn't at once reappear.

'I wonder what she's doing?' Pauline said. 'Perhaps she's washing out Alexey's handkerchief.'

'Or making us some more tea?' suggested Jean.

'Or finding another handkerchief for our Mum,' said Fergus. 'Look, her mouth is still bleeding. Do you think she is dying?' he asked, hopefully.

They looked down at her. Her cheeks still kept their colour, though they were pale compared with her mouth and chin.

'Don't be silly,' said Pauline. 'Of course she's not dying. People don't die from a smack in the face, do they, Mrs. Kirkwood?'

Mrs. Kirkwood was standing in the doorway.

'I couldn't tell you, I'm sure,' she said. 'I've never had one, we must wait and see. But I won't be messed about.' Her indignation had got the better of her. 'I won't be messed about,' she repeated. 'This was a respectable house once' – there were tears in her eyes – 'and now what are the neighbours going to say? And what are the lodgers I shall have to look for going to think, when they hear what's been going on here, as they certainly will? They'll think this house is a brothel.'

'The lodgers?' *inquired Pauline, with a rising inflexion in her voice, 'the* lodgers? *But you have Jean and Fergus'* – the children looked up and dried their eyes for a moment, at hearing their names mentioned. *'And you have Jock – when he's available. What other* lodgers *do you want?'*

'Oh, Miss Pauline,' replied Mrs. Kirkwood beginning [yes

beginning, Elizabeth III] *to clear away the tea-things, and the cakes which no one had so much as tasted. 'Leading the life you do, all fun and games, and Mr. Alexey too, not to mention Jock, though I don't quite know where he comes in – you wouldn't understand the problems of a working woman, and the need she has to keep herself to herself.'*

Pauline glanced down at Gina who was 'beginning', however unwillingly, to show signs of life.

'But I am a working woman, too, Mrs. Kirkwood! I work just as hard as you do! I know what it is to stand in bus-queues, and stay in lodgings much dingier than this – much dingier than this, Mrs. Kirkwood – and not know where my next meal is coming from.'

'And where is it coming from, Miss Pauline? From Jock, or Mr. Alexey, or who? For I don't believe you're all that good on the stage, you never have been and you never will be! But I don't have to depend on people like you, and the trouble they bring with them, and that's why –'

She broke down into hysterical sobbing and clutching at whatever support the furniture afforded, left the room.

'I think I'll go and talk to the children,' said Alexey, 'unless you'd rather, Jock. They look so wretched, huddled up together.'

'I'll say a word to them,' said Jock, striding across his wife's leather boots. 'But they'll have to get used to this sort of thing, if they're going to grow up.'

A glimpse of their thin uplifted arms, and the sound of Jock's smacking adult kisses, and his children's feeble, immature attempts, came from the corner.

'It'll do them good,' said Pauline to Alexey. 'Children like to be taken notice of. And it's nice to know that somebody likes somebody, and we don't all hate each other. What I don't understand is why Mrs. Kirkwood doesn't come back. Has she had a stroke, or something?'

'Perhaps she feels that her duties as a hostess are over,' said Alexey,

with unaccustomed acerbity. 'We have been rather a nuisance to her I suppose.'

'A nuisance?' echoed Pauline. 'A nuisance?' she repeated, as if such a thing where she was concerned, was unthinkable. 'But she gets well paid for it. I should think that any woman in her position would be only too thankful for a nuisance such as we are. She knows which side her bread is buttered, doesn't she?'

'Oh, my dearest Pauline,' said Alexey, forgetting how much the word 'dearest' grated on her, 'you can't argue that way.'

'I can, Alexey, and I do. Why doesn't she come out of her dirty kitchen, and tell us what's happening?'

'I don't think she wants to get mixed up in all this. I don't either – myself, I mean – but we have to accept what life sends.'

Pauline ignored this philosophical view of their predicament.

'And another thing, I don't understand,' she went on, as if in her case failure to understand constituted a virtue, 'is why Jock was driving this woman (she glanced down at the recumbent figure) about. Why were you, Jock?' she called across the room, interrupting the sound of Jock's clumsy, paternal endearments. 'You drove her to and fro in our car, as if you owned it, and then you go and hit her. It doesn't make sense. If you like a girl, you don't hit her.'

'Oh, don't you,' said Jock, 'that's all you know.'

They were standing, the three of them, in an uneven, uneasy circle, with the children between them, who sometimes looked up at them with puzzled faces and sometimes clasped Alexey's fingers, which he held out to them as a kind of benevolent bait.

'I know about her, of course,' went on Pauline, with a downward glance at the rhythmically moaning figure. 'I know that she ran away from you Jock, and took up with this nigger. Why? Was he better-looking than you, or better-off, or did he treat her better?'

'Pas devant les enfants,' warned Alexey, but neither Pauline nor Jock knew, or would have cared, what it meant.

'I don't know what he looked like,' said Jock, 'I never set eyes on him. *Those niggers all look much the same to me. I suppose she was meeting him from time to time, while I was out driving. She knew my times and dates, because I put them down on a bit of paper, over the kitchen sink, so as not to forget. She saw them and took advantage to meet this black fellow. And then she went off with him.*'

'*How long ago was that?*' Pauline demanded.

'*Oh, I dunno, quite a few years, perhaps.*' Jock obviously didn't want to commit himself. '*Anyhow, before I met you at the garage.*'

'*And then she got in touch with you, when the coloured gentleman was cooling off?*'

'*I don't exactly know why, but she wrote and said, Could we come together again, because of the children and everything. Children need a mum, don't they? A dad isn't the same, besides, I have to be out so much. Not that Mrs. Kirkwood hasn't been very good. So we met again, and tried to talk it over – I'm sorry I used your car, Mr. Alexey. It's a car that will take a bang, a good, solid, straight bang – but it was the easiest way and you had given me permission to use it.*'

'*Of course,*' Alexey said.

'*But not quite for those purposes, Alexey darling, not for love-making.*'

'*We didn't make love in it,*' said Jock, sharply.

'*Perhaps not, but still! – and she came here tonight to clinch matters?*'

Gina, on the carpet [in more senses than one, Elizabeth III] *rolled slightly to and fro.*

'*And what were you going to say, Jock?*'

'*Only this, Miss Pauline, Mr. Alexey, sir. I had no idea she was coming, and if I had been warned aforehand, I should have said, No. She wasn't here when I 'phoned.*'

'*So you would like things to go on as they were, Jock?*'

He paused for a long time. '*I don't know, I don't know. I may be in jug, and there's Mr. Alexey to consider.*'

'Don't worry about me,' Alexey said, giving Pauline a loving glance.

'No, sir, but you have been good to me, and I don't forget it. Nor do the children, do you?' He appealed to Jean and Fergus, who were trying to make a game for themselves as far away from Gina as the limited floor space allowed.

'Forget what?' asked Pauline, 'forget how kind, Grandad Alexey has been to you?'

'Oh, I never knew he was our grandad,' said Jean, and at that moment there was a knock on the door, the street door.

None of them answered it: they were all surprised into silence, even Jean and Fergus abandoned their abortive floor-game and stood up, while Mrs. Kirkwood's footsteps could be heard hurrying down the passage.

A moment later she opened the sitting-room door, followed by two policemen, holding their helmets in their hands, their ruddy, healthy faces looking ruddier and healthier from the cold outside.

'I understand you've had a spot of bother here, Mrs. Kirkwood?' said the sergeant, then noticing the body on the floor he added, 'Oh yes, I see.'

The others made way for him, and he knelt down and felt Gina's pulse – her eyes were still closed. 'Seems to be all right,' he said, 'but no doubt it's a case for an ambulance. Would you be so kind, Mrs. Kirkwood' (what a memory he has for names, thought Alexey, whose mind was roaming about) 'as to ring up 999 again, and they'll send an ambulance, pronto.'

'Yes, officer,' and Mrs. Kirkwood sped on her errand.

'And meanwhile,' said the sergeant almost jovially, not at all horrified or shocked, 'I'll just ask a few questions.' He glanced from face to face and Alexey said:

'There's a spot of whisky here, Sergeant. Would you and your colleague like some?'

The sergeant glanced at his companion, who nodded in a detached and non-committal way.

'Well, a spot of whisky is better than a spot of bother. It's against the regulations, but I won't say no,' said the sergeant expanding his expansive chest, 'and I dare say Bert here won't say no, either, being as it's such a cold night. But of course we must

thank Mrs. Kirkwood, when she comes back.' He looked at his watch. 'When she comes back,' he repeated, looking at his watch again.

Alexey did the duties of barman as to the manner born, for he was used to filling up his own and other people's glasses.

'You're not drinking yourselves, ladies and gentlemen?' asked the sergeant. 'Lady and gentlemen, I should say, since the lady on the floor seems to have passed out.' The others shook their heads, having no desire for conviviality; but Alexey, who never wanted to be out of step or out of tune, allowed himself a small swig.

'Good health,' said the sergeant, raising his glass. 'And specially,' he added humorously, 'to the lady at our feet.' Then his manner took on a more professional air. 'These questions, they're just routine questions, nothing to be afraid of.' His manner invited confidence, his voice was still cordial, but his eyes were sharp, 'All the same, I must warn you that your answers may be used in evidence. How did all this come about?' he asked, taking out his note-book, while his colleague, as though by a pre-arranged signal, took out his. 'Now sir,' turning to Alexey, 'can you give me an account of what led up to this unfortunate . . . accident? But perhaps we ought to clear the court; of the children, I mean. I don't suppose they come into it, do they?'

'Well, in a way they do,' said Jock, heavily. 'I'm their father, and she,' pointing to the ground, 'is their mother.'

'Oh really? Well, let's go into that later. Perhaps they could sit in the kitchen, with Mrs. Kirkwood.'

Towering above them, Jock took each by the hand and led them, protesting and casting backward glances towards the room. He was back in a trice, looking years older.

'And were you on good terms with your wife?' asked the sergeant.

'Oh, yes, while she was with me. She liked her comforts of course, but she was as snug as a bug in a rug, until this coloured fellow came along.'

129

'A coloured fellow?' asked the sergeant. 'And what did he do?'

'I don't know,' said Jock, 'but I know what she did. She ran off with him.'

'Racial discrimination?' said the sergeant, humorously. Seeing that Jock wasn't amused, he added:

'And were you fond of her, until this immigrant came along?'

'Oh yes, officer, I was. She had to go to hospital once, and I always went to see her. Some of them don't have any visitors at all. And before she came out I warmed up her clothes, especially her underwear.'

The sergeant made no comment, he had his own way of talking, as all policemen have. Turning to Alexey, he said:

'And you, sir, will you tell me how you come in?'

Steering clear of lies, which he knew would be fatal, Alexey explained as best he could. It was mortifying and humiliating: he had never before realized how indefensible was the role he had been playing. The sergeant however, didn't seem to think so; he noted the details as if they had been so much chicken-feed. And Pauline, too, was lucky; she tried to evade his questions once or twice, but it was clear that he admired her, as a woman, and thought her behaviour hardly deviated from the normal. Jock had a worse time in trying to answer the sergeant's questions, correct and impersonal though they were.

'So you don't know why you hit the lady on the carpet?' asked the sergeant. 'It was a bit of a tiff, I expect, quite usual between husbands and wives.'

Jock couldn't trust himself to speak, especially in the presence of Alexey, their benefactor. He must know about it, thought Jock. But he had to answer.

'Oh yes,' he said, 'we had a few words. Women, you know.'

The sergeant gave him an understanding smile.

Their three tales told, and each one's shame in its different measure partially revealed, they looked round for somewhere to sit down.

Actually, besides the sofa and its flanking armchairs, the three-piece suite, there were two 'occasional' chairs, which could have been used during the interrogation. They hadn't been used, because neither Mrs. Kirkwood nor her guests realized how tired they were, until the sergeant stopped questioning them. Now they looked round for support for their backs and their backsides; even Jock was glad to perch precariously on the edge of a high chair intended for a child.

Pauline subsided on to the sofa; Alexey looked about and said, 'Where will you sit, Sergeant?'

'Don't worry about me,' said the sergeant, who perhaps, thanks to the whisky, looked even fresher than when he came into the room, 'and that goes for my pal, too. We're used to standing, ha-ha!'

'Well, sit down all the same,' said Alexey, planting himself beside Pauline on the sofa. The policemen disposed themselves on the vacant chairs, and Gina had the floor to herself.

While the sergeant was completing his notes, the three culprits, as they knew themselves to be, experienced a few moments of revulsion mixed with relief. None of them had anything to be proud of; but for the time being all was over. They were like fishes, dead on the fishmongers' slab. A few hours before, a few minutes before, they had been gay and lively, sporting in the sea with all the freedom of the sea; now they had been hooked or netted, and their carefree life was over. They were exposed, exposed in their nakedness to the eye of the law. Who would want them? Who would want even to look at a dead fish, unless it was eatable, which they were not.

The sergeant raised his eyes from his note-book. 'There's just one more question I'd like to ask, it's only a matter of routine. Would Mrs. Kirkwood be available? Bert, just go into the kitchen, and ask her to come in for a moment. Perhaps one of you would look after the children. We don't want to upset them!'

Jock jumped up, and accompanied Bert to the kitchen.

'Yes?' said Mrs. Kirkwood, standing in the doorway, with Bert's uniform and bright buttons and medals making a background for her. 'You wanted to speak to me?'

Does the house belong to me or you? she seemed to be saying.

'Please sit down, Madam,' said the sergeant, who had risen at her entrance. 'The three witnesses have answered my questions very fairly, and I can say I know the whole set-up – it isn't a very uncommon one.' (He sighed.) 'I haven't asked the lady on the floor – that will come later. I don't think that what she says will make a material difference to my conclusions.' He looked down at Gina, whose eyes flickered and then closed. 'But what I should like to ask you is why you rang us up instead of the ambulance? We policemen have a lot to do, and if every little quarrel in a household –'

'I have my good name to think of, officer,' said Mrs. Kirkwood. 'This is a respectable house, not a disorderly house, and I wanted to have my name cleared.'

'Quite, quite,' said the sergeant, placably. 'And we shall do our best to clear it for you when . . . when the lady at our feet has come round. But I presume you knew what the situation was, you knew, for instance, who was paying for the room and the children's keep?'

'Jock paid. He's earning good money.'

'No doubt he is. But come, come, Mrs. Kirkwood, could he have paid for the children, and the room, at the price you are asking, without outside help?'

'How do you know what price I am asking?' demanded Mrs. Kirkwood with her hand on the door-knob.

The sergeant, facing her, shrugged his shoulders. 'Don't run away, Mrs. Kirkwood. It stands to sense, doesn't it? You would have been better advised, if you wanted to keep this business quiet, being an indoor job, to have called an ambulance instead of us. We policemen have plenty on our plates, without attending to a woman who seems to be a roughy-toughy type, who has got a few of her teeth knocked in.'

'I didn't know they'd let you have an ambulance unless you first informed the police,' said Mrs. Kirkwood, sticking to her guns.

'Well, you know now,' said the sergeant.

'Yes, I do know,' retorted Mrs. Kirkwood, 'since you say so, but I think it would help us women, who take in lodgers, and sometimes get taken in by them, to know where we stand. It will be a police-court case, won't it?'

'It will either be assault and battery or disturbing the peace,' said the sergeant, with a shrug. 'People in lodging-houses are always beating each other up – it just depends on how far they go.'

'What do you mean by that?' demanded Mrs. Kirkwood.

'Nothing whatever, but people are people, all the world over.'
He paused.

'Ah, there's the ambulance.'

No one but he had heard it drawing up.

The men came in. Expertly lifting Gina from the carpet, they carried her van-wards.

'We must go, too,' said the sergeant, and he and his aide bowed themselves out.

'And we must go too, mustn't we, Alexey?' said Pauline. 'I feel I've been here several days, not just a few hours. What a smell those policemen left! But we can't go without Jock: where is he?'

'I'll go and look,' Alexey said. Soon he returned with Jock, the children dancing at his side.

'Have they all gone?' said Jean in a tone of bitter disappointment. 'And we wanted to talk to them so much, didn't we, Fergus? Especially the policemen. We've never seen a policeman to talk to, have we, Granny? And there were those other men who came in that great big car to take our Mum away (you didn't know that we were looking, but we were). Is she going to die, do you think?' Jean who knew nothing of death except its publicity-value, spoke as hopefully of her mother's decease as Fergus had.

'Of course not,' snapped Pauline. 'People don't die of a smack in the mouth.'

'Then will she come back and be our Mum? She's so pretty – she's prettier than you are, Miss Pauline, except of course she wants her face doing up.'

No one said anything to this.

The excitement of the drama over, they were each thinking what effect it would have on their daily lives.

'But she'll have to come back, won't she,' pursued Jean, 'if Dad goes to prison?'

'Time will show,' said Jock gruffly, 'you shut up, Jean, we've had enough of you.'

CHAPTER XII

Well, dearest Elizabeth, I have read and re-read your letter and I have read the chapters you referred to. You will not be surprised to hear that I agree with everything you said, especially with the reservations! I will return to them later.

You told me you were puzzled by the ending of the book – not by what *happened*, which you said was fairly clear, but the construction, or to put it more magniloquently, the interpretation that I put on it.

I'm not sure that I put any interpretation on it, and yet if you were to ask me, 'Was that what *really* happened?' I should hesitate to say yes. It is a platitude that truth is stranger than fiction: truth has to be groomed, twisted, perhaps turned upside-down, to be acceptable in a novel. The *Iliad* and the *Odyssey* are most carefully constructed novels; Homer, or whoever he was, had his eye on the last page when he wrote the first. They work up to a climax: even the *Odyssey* does, though it is essentially a picaresque, episodic novel, without the continuous development of plot that the *Iliad* has. Of all the novelists comparable to Homer in stature, only Cervantes, I think, *improvises* the ending. *Don Quixote* is not *constructed*, according to any canons of art; it doesn't work up to anything; it hasn't a dénouement or a climax, the logical issue of what has gone before, unless Don Quixote's disillusion with Dulcinea (which no doubt was always in the author's mind) could be counted as an anti-climax. Don Quixote's death, moving as it is, and perfectly in harmony with his unstressed religious faith – the faith which, though he may have been unaware of it, upheld him through all his adventures – this is just thrown in at the end, as the average man's or woman's death is, without sound and fury, but as far as the purpose and pattern of their lives are concerned – as a final statement of what they meant to be, and what they were meant to be – signifying nothing. Or does it signify something?

But what was I trying to say, darling Elizabeth? I only wish you were here to remind me! When I had to decide how to finish off Pauline and Alexey and Jock and Gina (and Jean and Fergus for they couldn't be left out), I tried to make a compromise between what would have befallen them in the police-court world, and *justice. Fiat justitia! Fiat justitia!* You know the old saying, 'Whoever accepts a gift, pays a forfeit?' Well, they had all accepted gifts, Pauline from Alexey, Alexey in a rather roundabout way from Pauline, Jock from both of them, and the children had, although they didn't realize it. Mrs. Kirkwood, although she would have been the last to admit it, had also received gifts – a comfortable salary in return for her care of Jean and Fergus (which was really a labour of love). Only Gina had given nothing (except to her coloured boyfriend) and received nothing (except a smack in the mouth from Jock). I found it hard to fit her into my idea of justice. At the most she had only lost a few teeth (which weren't her own, anyhow) and Jock's Counsel (for whom Alexey paid) made great play with the fact that she forsook him and their children for a Negro. What more natural than that Jock should try to find consolation (if he did, which as Counsel pointed out, was far from proved) elsewhere, and the means of supporting his children elsewhere? At the worst, his attack on Gina was a *crime passionnel*, and could readily be excused on grounds of diminished responsibility.

When I see you again, which I hope will be very soon after

your sad vigil is over, may we return to the questions you raised about my novel, and particularly to the matter and manner of the ending?

Finis coronat opus: In my end is my beginning; and it is even truer for the novelist, that in my beginning is my end. But in order to defend it, or just to explain it, I must re-read it – a hateful task, which I would undertake for no one but you – and tell myself exactly what happened. What I wrote then I may utterly disown now. Writing is a continuous process, a long journey into unexplored country, with many stops and 'diversions' on the way, and the end attained is not always the end one aimed at. *Littera scripta manet:* it is too late to change what I wrote, but not too late to think what I might have written. If we had collaborated, either literally or through the interchange of our imaginations (but yours was inaccessible then, and no wonder!) the outcome might have been different.

How pretentious this sounds!

And now I am going to refresh my memory, which I suspect is not as good as yours (for my memory clamps down on what I have recently written) of the last chapters.

Your loving James

Gina had given Jock ample provocation, both by deed and word. Some people in the court sympathized with her because of her beauty – she was at least ten years younger than Pauline, and fair instead of dark, which told in her favour, and there were some who thought that racial discrimination told against her because her fancy-man was coloured.

But on the whole she didn't come out of the proceedings very well. She had left Jock and her children because she was tired of them; and the black man who, incidentally, could not be found, but whose name was Achille, had left her because he was tired of her. He had made no attempt to support her children, although, when she appeared in court it seemed possible, and even probable, that he had at least given her a child.

She was granted legal aid, and her line, when cross-examined was, this is what I am, and this is what nature does to us. But these arguments didn't cut much ice with the jury, nor did her mouth, which was still disfigured by the impact of Jock's knuckles – for after all, broken dentures (though just as expensive to replace) don't arouse so much compassion as do broken teeth.

Alexey's examination was less embarrassing than he expected. He was a well-to-do, middle-aged man who, as such men will, had attached himself to Pauline with the view of making life easier and pleasanter for her – and for himself, although this aspect of their relationship was not stressed. It was however, made clear – and it told as much in her favour as in his – that she had never encouraged the friendship. 'Mr. Alexey has been kind to me,' she said, 'and I value his kindness, and I always shall, but there have been times –'

'What sort of times, Mrs. Merryweather?' asked the magistrate.

'Oh, sir, how can I explain?' and Pauline's face went through the range of expressions which had made her, as an actress, the considerable success that she was. 'Mr. Alexey has always been most kind and considerate, he has gone out of his way –' she waved her hand, half to the magistrate, half to the handful of people in the court. 'He has gone out of his way to do me favours that I would never, never have asked of him. Favours that I did not always want.'

'I think I understand,' said the magistrate who, despite himself, could not quite resist the attraction of this man-adaptable, man-adapted, woman, 'I think I understand.'

'As for Mr. Campbell and myself,' she went on, 'we shared . . . we shared so many things together. But there was nothing, nothing whatever, between us that could have made his wife jealous.'

'You were fond of his children?' asked the magistrate, casually.

'Oh yes, it was on account of them, and Mr. Jock Campbell's natural wish to see them, that we went to Mrs. Kirkwood's house. I didn't want to go,' lied Pauline, 'I was all against it, but I was over-ruled.'

'By whom?' the magistrate asked.

'By them, by Jock, and Mr. Alexey and so on. We didn't expect to find Mrs. Campbell there – it was quite a shock, I can assure you.'

'Mrs. Kirkwood?'

'I have nothing much to say, sir. My conscience is quite clear. I did my best by the children – they are nice little kids, I will say that – but I had no idea, no idea whatsoever, until I came into Court, that part of the money for their board and lodging came from Mr. Alexey. I knew of course, that Mr. Campbell and his wife were separated, but that was no business of mine, and as soon as I saw how she was acting up and Jock thumped her, I left the room and called the police. And I didn't come back until the police came. I don't want to be mixed up with things of that sort!'

'It does you credit, Mrs. Kirkwood.'

'I am glad to hear you say so, sir,' rejoined Mrs. Kirkwood, the red of moral indignation flaming on her cheeks – 'and it does a woman no good, especially a widow like me, to lose their good name because of a lot of unknown layabouts, who push themselves in without being asked.'

Mrs. Kirkwood rummaged in her bag and took out her handkerchief.

'There, there, Mrs. Kirkwood,' said the chairman. 'We all sympathize with you.'

'Sympathy is not enough, sir,' said Mrs. Kirkwood, 'I think I ought to be indemnified.'

'Indemnified, Mrs. Kirkwood?' The chairman wondered who had put this word into her head.

'Yes, sir, indemnified, given the equivalent in money of what I've suffered in grief and pain, and the loss of my good name.'

The chairman glanced at his colleagues.

'I don't think anyone will question your good name, unless you question it yourself.'

Mrs. Kirkwood sniffed. 'That's as may be, sir. And when this present lot have been cleaned out – I say cleaned out, because chauffeurs and their children aren't all that clean, I shall have to look about for people who are as particular as I am.'

The preliminary case was over and Jock got off very lightly, being discharged with a caution. Three cars stood outside the magistrate's court, three for the four people mainly concerned. Other witnesses had been called, but not being themselves involved in the action, they had told the truth and nothing but the truth. They were left to make their own get-away as best they could.

Alexey stood looking at the three cars, and turned up the collar of his overcoat, for it was still chilly. For the first time in this quadri-lateral relationship, it was for him to decide. He didn't relish it; he didn't like power, except when modified, diluted, transformed, or whatever, in terms of love. Naked power, the chief agent in the world to-day, had never appealed to him. And decision was even more abhorrent to him, but the other three were waiting for him – and he had to make his mind up.

The three cars he had ordered were standing outside: but the placements, *the* placements! *Who should go in each?*

Conscious of being the least glamorous of the quartet, he approached the blonde-haired Gina, so much his junior.

'Gina, will you take this car and go wherever you want to go, and send me the account?'

'Yes, Mr. Alexey, but I shall want to know about the children – and other things, too.'

'We'll discuss that later.'

Before the uniformed chauffeur had time to open the door for her, Alexey had opened it, and the car slowly started off.

Looking round he espied a fifth figure, standing at the back of the group, and evidently wanting to dissociate herself from them, except for the convenience of transport.

'Stop! stop!' he shouted, as far as he was able to shout. The chauffeur pulled up. 'Mrs. Kirkwood,' he apologized, 'I had forgotten about you. Please share the car with Gina, and whichever of you comes first – I mean, whose destination comes first – well, settle it between yourselves.'

The two women glared at each other, as if any kind of settlement was unthinkable. But Mrs. Kirkwood was already at the door, and the car moved off for the second time.

'Wait for me, will you?' said Alexey with a hasty glance at Jock, who in his correct navy-blue suit and black tie, was resting his hand passively, and affectionately, on the wing of the Austin Princess. 'Wait for me, will you? I want a word with Miss Pauline.'

'You want a word with me, do you?' asked Pauline, who had overheard this and most of the rest of the conversation. 'You want a word, just a word?'

'Let's discuss it later,' said Alexey, in extreme agitation. 'I do feel that at this point, at this stage, as they say, it would be better for both of us if we weren't seen together. I'm sure you will understand.'

'Better for you perhaps, you have nothing to lose.'

'Only you,' said Alexey. 'But I've lost you already.'

'Oh Alexey,' said Pauline, 'how can you attach so much importance to what is said by a pack of nobodies in a law-court?'

'It isn't only that,' Alexey said. 'I know I am stupid, but –'

'But what?'

'I don't feel you are the same person that I used to know.'

He moved towards the Austin Princess, and never had he been more glad to see any door opened.

'I shan't go until you go,' Pauline called after him. 'I shan't go until you go.'

He saw her car, with the window drawn down, ready to say something [oh dear, Elizabeth III], she called, she shouted, she waved; she made the frantic, inward-turning gestures of someone who has lost something of vital importance. But Alexey said to

Jock, who was driving Alexey's car, 'Drive on, we can't wait any longer.'

'You don't want to speak to Miss Pauline, sir?'

'Well, not at this moment.'

They drove on in silence until they came to the cross-roads. Jock slowed up.

'Where to now, sir?'

'I thought I'd go to my flat in London.'

'Very good, sir.' Jock had ceased to refer, and defer, to his hydra-headed employer. 'But what about your things?'

'My things, Jock?'

'Yes sir, your bits and pieces. They must be at the West Riding Hotel, where you and where we – spent the night.'

'Oh, I don't think I mind about them.'

'It would be a pity to leave them,' said Jock, 'especially in these days, when hair-brushes and such-like are so expensive. It's only a few miles out of the way. You needn't go to the hotel yourself sir, if you don't want to, there's a pub near by, where you could be quite comfortable for twenty minutes, while I'm collecting your goods and chattels.'

'Its very kind of you, Jock,' Alexey said, 'let's do that.'

'Of course you could have your personal effects sent back to you, but it might take time.' Jock often said the same thing twice.

'You are quite right, Jock.'

'Only I should have to have some money, to pay your bill at the hotel, I mean – that is, unless you've already paid it.'

'Thank you for reminding me. And perhaps somebody would like a tip.'

He gave Jock some money, and they sped along until a beam of artificial light pierced the natural twilight of the Yorkshire Dale.

'Here it is,' said Jock, 'The Scroby Arms. I'll be back in a jiffy.'

.   .   .

How long is a jiffy? Alexey asked himself, sitting in the bar with the companionship of a large whisky. It was called 'The Brontë Bar', and there was a reproduction of Branwell's now famous portrait of his three sisters.

Branwell was a great pub-crawler, if not great in any other way. Desperately trying to keep his thoughts at bay, Alexey remembered the problems of the Brontë family, which were so much worse than his. He didn't succeed.

. . .

What a long journey it would be to London, four hours or more, with nothing to look forward to and nothing but mistakes to look back on. For Pauline had been a mistake, a colossal mistake; he realized that now. She had entered into the emptiness of his life, with all her fullness of being, only to leave it emptier. She would find a substitute for him, no doubt; she might have found one already. But would he ever find a substitute for her, someone who would undertake, however unwillingly, the whole weight of his emotional personality, his every-day letters, his constant telephone-calls, his insistence that she, busy as she was, should share every moment of her life with him? Someone who would accept, without demur, the money he had so lavishly poured out on Pauline, every penny of which must have cost her a sense of obligation she was unable to fulfil?

No wonder she had turned to Jock, with his good looks and his thews and sinews, who made no demands on her, who was probably slightly bored by her, except in so far as it gave him a certain status to drive her about. And he had something to offer her – though goodness knows if she appreciated it – which he, Alexey, had not: a life that was up against life, a variousness and richness of experience which didn't show much, because Jock wouldn't let it show, but which was there all the same, giving force to his silences, and his occasional utterances, behind the driving-wheel. His wife had left him; he had two children; experience had ridden rough-shod over him, and he had imparted it to her – who knew how, or how often?

One thing was certain: he, Alexey could not see her any more. She was a different person from the one his imagination, his besotted imagination, had conjured up. She might be someone else's, but she wasn't his. And just as his mind, and his will-power, and his common-sense (for after all he had it, in business at any rate) had not broken him of his infatuation, so, once it was broken, not all the King's horses and all the King's men could put it together again. For it didn't depend on friendship, which is more or less amenable to reason and to the dictates of the conscious mind, it depended on love, which is not.

She was no longer his Pauline: she was anyone: he felt he would hardly have recognized her if he saw her.

So he could not feel for Pauline, dethroned, even the most ordinary obligations of friendship. He had indeed hired a car to take her back to her hotel after the trial, but he could not have answered when, at the moment of parting, she leaned out of the window and waved and called his name again and again, with a rising inflection of appeal that was like a wail.

.   .   .

'Be absolute for love!'

Once a man, or a woman, for that matter, has tasted the heady brew of a strong personal attachment, especially in middle-age, it becomes a necessity, an addiction. Alexey's previous relationships with women had been fleeting and unsatisfactory: he could not equate love with sex. While he was with Pauline, the need for loving was paramount with him, it made secondary, or less than secondary, the need for sex.

But Nature, which abhors a vacuum, is only too fertile in finding objects of adoration, or sacrifice, or both, to fill it. The 'aching void' as it is conventionally but correctly called, simply must be filled.

The car drew up into the courtyard of the Scroby Arms, so much ampler than the meagre parking-space allotted to those who were summoned to the Magistrates' Court. Pleasure before business! Alexey was sitting beside Jock now, not in the back seat which he generally occupied with or without Pauline, who preferred to sit in the front. The Scroby Arms was a half-way house to the hotel where he had been staying with Pauline. He couldn't face the possibility of meeting her there, so he asked Jock to go ahead and collect his things, while he himself waited three miles away – a safe distance.

Jock, who knew the Scroby Arms well, escorted him, taking his arm as if he was in need of support to the entrance of the hotel. 'The bar's on the left,' he said, in a pregnant whisper: he might have been indicating the location of the Holy Grail. 'I'll be back with you in . . . in a very short time.'

.   .   .

At last, his head outlined against the neon-lighting of the Brontë Bar Jock re-appeared, carrying two suitcases and something draped over his shoulders.

The drapery turned out to be Alexey's dressing-gown.

'I couldn't get it in, sir,' he explained, panting, 'in the short time there was, and I had quite a set-to with the man at the desk, because he wanted to charge you for an extra day, because you hadn't evacuated your room by twelve o'clock. I said "Nonsense, you won't get any more customers today," which was quite obvious, being as the hotel is only half-full. He was quite unpleasant about it! And then he said, "What about Miss Pauline Merryweather? Who is paying for her? Mr. Alexey engaged two rooms, one for him and one for her." So I said, "Mr. Alexey is paying for her room," and I gave him the money, sir, I happened to have it on me.'

'You were quite right, Jock.'

'And I also paid for my room, which was in another part of the building, where they don't charge so much.'

'You were quite right, Jock.'

'The fiver you gave me didn't quite cover it, sir, not with the tips and so on, which you asked me to give, in case you should go there again.'

'You were quite right, Jock. I must owe you quite a lot of money.'

'Don't worry about that, sir, I've kept the account.' He half produced it from his pocket, and then put it back. 'But there's one thing more, Mr. Alexey, sir.'

'What is that?'

'It's the key of your bedroom-door, the one next to Miss Pauline's. They want to know if you've got it.'

'Good God!'

Alexey searched his pocket, all his pockets, and brought out the key.

'You won't be wanting it now, sir?'

'Of course not.'

'Then I'll take it back to them. They says it costs them a small fortune, the keys that customers take away, and don't return. I'll be back in a jiffy.'

This jiffy was shorter than the last.

'All's in order now, Mr. Alexey. Everything's under control.'

'Well, shall we start for London?'

The Austin Princess began to purr.

Alexey felt sleepy. The events of the day, and of the days before, had tired him; thoughts that he had tried to keep at bay had tired him too.

'*Where are we now, Jock?*'

'*We're approaching Newark, sir.*'

'*Isn't that nearly half-way?*'

'*Half-way, sir?*'

'*Half-way to London, I meant.*'

'*Oh yes, another three hours, with luck.*'

'*You must be tired,*' *said Alexey, attributing to Jock his own sensations.*

'*Oh no, sir,*' *said Jock, affronted at the idea.* '*I'm never tired.*'

'*You must be hungry, then,*' *said Alexey, determined to discover some need that Jock had, and if necessary to create one. How many needs, hitherto dormant or unimagined, had he created for Pauline?*

'*Well, sir,*' *said Jock,* '*I won't say no to that. To tell you the truth,*' *he added, as if the truth was something indecent to tell,* '*I do feel a bit peckish.*'

'*Let's stop at Peterborough, then.*'

'*We don't go through Peterborough, not on the direct route. Normancross, perhaps?*'

'*Yes, Normancross.*'

Alexey dozed again. He tried to reconcile himself to his new personality, his naked personality, himself without Pauline. Often as she had told him, in moments of irritation (for she was, according to her lights, an honest woman), that he was following a false scent, and barking up the wrong tree, he wouldn't believe it. He thought that because he was in love with her, she must be in love with him.

Jock, with his hands on the steering-wheel and his eyes peering into the darkness of the A.1, knew more about Pauline than he did. Jock's wife had said so, and possibly it was so.

Oddly enough, it didn't make Alexey angry with Jock: Jock, he felt, had been his deputy, and had given her something that her feeling for him, Alexey, had made unacceptable. Long ago he had suspected this and fought against the suspicion: he didn't believe it because he didn't want to believe it. Perish the thought.

'Coming into Normancross now, sir.'

Alexey blinked. 'I must have fallen asleep. Let's order some dinner.'

'I'll just park the car first, sir.'

Why were there always these practical considerations?

Coming back Jock asked, 'Would you rather dine alone, Mr. Alexey, sir? There's another room where the chauffeurs go, it's quite good.'

Would Jock rather be on his own, Alexey wondered, with his own kind, where he could relax and spread his elbows out, and put his knife and fork facing each other on the plate?

'No, I'd rather we dined together, if you don't mind.'

'Then I'll engage a table,' said Jock promptly.

'You'll find me in the bar,' Alexey said.

Their aperitifs should have made things easier, but after the meal had been ordered, a steak for Jock and a grilled sole for him, Alexey didn't know what to say, and it was Jock who started the conversation.

'I'm sorry about this, I'm sorry, very sorry, Mr. Alexey. You've behaved like a gentleman, I can't say more.'

He had already finished his steak, while Alexey was still toying with his sole.

'Have another helping?'

'I won't say no.'

While it was on order, and while Alexey was wondering whether he would be able to finish his sole, he asked:

'Did you see Miss Pauline at the hotel, Jock?

'I did, sir. I went up to your room, to pack your bits and pieces – the man at the desk didn't want me to, he was quite unpleasant because I hadn't paid the bill, so I paid it, and then he let me go. But I told you that!'

'You must tell me how much it was.'

Jock hesitated.

'Well, yes, Mr. Alexey. I've got the receipts as I told you. It wasn't all that much, my room being in another part of the building.'

'And you saw Miss Pauline?'

'Yes, I did happen to see her.'

At this moment the second portion of steak arrived, with all its garnishings, and Jock looked at it, with a still hungry eye.

'It was like this, sir,' he resumed, when his knife and fork were well dug into the steak, 'I dropped into the bar to have a quick one, while the porter was bringing down your suitcase – I gave him half-a-dollar for doing that.'

'You were quite right, Jock. Here's the half-crown.' He took one out of his pocket, and steered it towards Jock, under the upturned edges of intervening plates. A miniature commando manœuvre, to get it to its goal without being seen.

But Jock shook his head.

'No, Mr. Alexey, no sir, I'd rather not. You've done a lot for me, only it was just in case we came back again –'

'To the hotel, you mean? I doubt if we shall.'

'No, but one never knows, and the staff will remember if you've seen them, money-wise, I mean.'

'I'm sure you're right.'

'Well, I popped into the bar while he was taking your baggage down. I brought my own down, and I put it in the boot of the car and left it unlocked for him – perhaps I was wrong, but you have to trust people sometimes.'

'Quite right, Jock.'

'Well, I went into the bar, and there was Miss Pauline, sitting on a stool with her head resting on the bar. I thought she was a bit tiddly, if you know what I mean, and women are quicker to show it than men are. I mean they give way to their feelings quicker. So I just asked for a pint of bitter, and went to the opposite corner where I thought she couldn't see me. But she lifted her head up and saw me – she wasn't tiddly, she was just crying.'

'What happened then?'

'Oh, she got off the stool and came and sat beside me on the bench, I suppose you would call it a settee, well-padded, very posh. And she said, between her sobs, "Where are you off to now?" Everyone looked round, but she didn't seem to care – I suppose women are like that.'

'And what did you say, Jock?'

'I told her the truth, Mr. Alexey. I told her the truth. I said I was driving you back to London. "And can't you take me with you, Jock," she asked, "can't you take me with you?"'

'That was rather a facer, but I said, "I can't take you with me now, because I don't know what Mr. Alexey's plans are, and he is my employer, in a manner of speaking."'

' "Is he here now?" she asked.

'Then I told her the truth. I said, "He's not exactly here. He's some way off, on the A.1, and I've got to pick him up." And I looked at the wrist-watch that you gave me, sir.'

'Did Miss Pauline ever give you anything, Jock?'

'Oh yes, she gave me a few things but I couldn't think about them then, because I knew you were waiting. So I offered her a drink, but *she wouldn't have it, and I didn't like to say more, because half the people in the bar seemed to recognize her – they recognize almost anyone who's been on T.V. – they would recognize you or me, sir – so I just said, "All the best, and thanks for everything, and I'll be seeing you" and I got up and left. She was still crying, but what else could I do? Women's tears come very easily – it's not like with us men.'*

Jock was already half-way through his second steak, while Alexey was still fiddling with his sole.

'And what do you propose to do now?'

'Drive you to London, sir,' answered Jock, surprised.

'Yes, and after that?'

At last Alexey had put the ball into Jock's court.

'After that, sir, I hadn't really thought. Working class men like me can't look far ahead. We have to take it as it comes, if you know what I mean. I can always get a job in a garage.'

'In the same garage?'

'Good God no, sir, if you will excuse the expression. I shouldn't mind for myself, my back's quite broad enough. But I should mind for the kids' sakes, Jean and Fergus. They would have a hell of a time, after the publicity there's been in the Press, and may be again, just because I thumped that damned bitch –'

'But Mrs. Kirkwood –'

'Oh, you heard what she said. I've paid her good money, or to be fair, you have. She wouldn't be so kind to them now. But that wouldn't matter. It's something else.'

'What is it, then?'

'It's the other school-children, sir. They'd give mine hell. Perhaps you don't know what school-children are like –'

'Oh yes, I do.'

'They're little devils. It's enough for them to know that your middle name, if you have one, is odd – I'm called Jock Maconochie Campbell – and they give you no peace, no peace at all. I was big and

strong for my age, so I didn't suffer much, but they used to shout after me "Maconochie, Maconochie", and I used to run home crying.'

'Children can be very brutal,' said Alexey, lamely.

'Yes, sir, and how much worse would it be for them, my kids, I mean, after the newspaper reports? "Your dad's a so-and-so, your mum's a so-and-so?" Why, they'd be driven up the wall. They'd grow up to be mixed-up kids, or delinquents, or worse. Oh, no, Mr. Alexey, I shan't leave them there. I know it's my fault, in a manner of speaking, and you know too, but why should they suffer?'

'Why should any of us suffer?' asked Alexey.

'Well, sir, we're bound to suffer, that's the way of it. But we needn't suffer more than we need, and that's why I'm going to take the children away.'

'Where are you going to take them, Jock?'

'I haven't had time to think it out,' said Jock, 'it's all happened so suddenly. It needn't have happened if Miss Pauline –'

'Yes, I know she was always self-willed,' replied Alexey, who now thought as well as spoke of Pauline in the past tense.

'I did give her a broad hint, didn't I, not to go into Mrs. Kirkwood's place while my wife was there?'

'You did indeed. But if you had told her your wife was there, she could have wanted to go all the more.'

'I don't understand women,' said Jock. The drink, and the food and the warmth, and the momentary relief from anxiety, had loosened his tongue. 'You'd think that she'd have known that she was sitting pretty, on velvet, I might almost say. There was you, Mr. Alexey, and there was me, if I may mention myself, and we were all getting on well together, and yet she has to bust it all up.'

'Well, let's be fair to her,' said Alexey, pushing away the last fragment of his sole. 'It was your wife who really bust it up.'

'You're right,' said Jock, 'you're absolutely right, sir. But she's another woman, isn't she?'

Alexey couldn't deny this.

'And they don't know how, they don't know how – how shall I put it? To keep the status quo.

After Jock had had an ice, which Alexey refused, they ordered coffee, and while it was coming Alexey said:

'But you haven't told me what you mean to do now.'

'I don't rightly know myself, sir. But I shall find a job somewhere, perhaps somewhere in the South. I've always had a fancy for the South. Lots of Scotsmen feel that way.'

Alexey remembered Dr. Johnson's dictum that the best thing a Scotsman ever saw was the road to England.

'But what about the children?'

'Oh, I shall find a place for them,' Jock didn't sound over confident. 'Besides, I might get married again. I could get a divorce on the grounds of desertion.'

'Are you sure?' asked Alexey, stirring his coffee. 'I don't know how long – how many years – legally constitutes desertion. And she came back to you anyway.'

'Yes, she did, blast her.' Jock suddenly looked hunted and tired, and as if he wanted to escape from the room. 'It's a hard life for a married man, you wouldn't know, being a bachelor, Mr. Alexey, if I may say so.'

Alexey called for the bill, and while it was coming he again asked Jock:

'What are your immediate plans?'

'My immediate plan is to drive you to London.'

'And then?'

'Then I shall drive back to Yorkshire to see how the bairns are.'

'You mean tonight?'

'Yes, Mr. Alexey, it's quicker driving at night.'

'You must be mad,' said Alexey, giving a note to the waiter, 'Now

F*   155

please, Jock, take my advice. Ring up Mrs. Kirkwood – it's only half past eight, she won't be in bed – and say you will be coming to see her sometime, perhaps tomorrow, perhaps later.'

'But today's Thursday,' objected Jock, 'and I haven't paid the rent.'

'Oh don't bother about the rent,' said Alexey, with the indifference of the well-to-do to the preoccupations of the poor. 'Don't bother about the rent – say you have a present for her from me.'

'You're very kind, Mr. Alexey.'

When Jock was pleased he bent forward and a kind of glow shone behind his eyes, whether physical or emotional it would be hard to say.

The waiter came back with the change. Alexey didn't notice how large his tip was, but Jock did and shook his head.

'You spoil people, you know, Mr. Alexey.'

'Oh, what does it matter? But you must go and telephone.'

'Yes, Mr. Alexey, but could you lend me a tanner or two?' he asked, with his eyes on the change on the table. 'They want such funny sums nowadays, you never have the right amount in your pocket, when you call from a kiosk.'

'Take what you like,' said Alexey, pushing the coins towards him.

'Oh no,' said Jock, 'two and threepence will be enough.'

He carefully counted out the cash, and left.

What a long tiring day! Alexey dozed, his head nodded, and though he was aware that he ought ['ought', Elizabeth III 'ought?'] to maintain a proper deportment in the Normancross Hotel, he wondered if he would be able to. His chin, dropping almost painfully with a sudden jerk on his chest, kept waking him. Finally fatigue overcame him, and he slept with the complete sleep that obliterates the sense of time. So that Jock might have been away a year, instead of a few minutes, when his shadow, darkening the light on the table-cloth, woke Alexey up.

'Oh, it's you, Jock,' he said, still confused.

Jock smiled.

'Yes, sir, it's me, but I haven't any good news.'

He looked very crestfallen.

'Tell me the worst,' Alexey said, putting a brave if sleepy front on Jock's troubles.

'It's like this, sir, Gina, that's my wife, has been to see Mrs. Kirkwood and told her what she means to do – take the kids away, claim restitution of conjugal rights – she called it 'congenial nights', not being well-educated – and sue me for maintenance.'

By now Alexey was wide-awake.

'Oh, I doubt if she can. It would cost her too much, for one thing. Besides, she has been living in adultery with this Negro.'

He paused and invited Jock to sit down.

'I don't want to say it,' said Jock, 'but since you know it already, I will. They could say that Miss Pauline and I have been close friends. How my wife found out, I don't know.'

He looked unutterably depressed.

'Well, cheer up,' said Alexey, who was far from feeling cheerful himself, 'cheer up, and let's look on the bright side. The court may say that as she came back to you within a statutory period –'

'That was just a trick, sir.'

'Yes, but still. . . . The law favours the mother in such cases, and if she really wants to have the children back –'

'I don't think she does, sir, and how can she support them?'

'The State would help her, and she could get a part-time job, I suppose.'

'A bed-time job is all she's good for,' said Jock bitterly. 'Otherwise she's no more use than a sick headache.'

'Then what do you propose to do?'

Jock paused.

'Either marry Miss Pauline, she wants me to, so she says, or dodge about, as many blokes in my situation do, dodge about from one place to another, leaving no address, so they can't fix a maintenance charge on me. That's what I'd better do. I don't think it would work out if I married Miss Pauline. It was different when we had . . . when we had you, sir, to back us up, or to fall back on, if you know what I mean.'

A deep shade of red wattled Jock's swarthy countenance, and he bent his head forwards, showing the slight tonsure, where his hair was beginning to thin [yes, beginning to thin, Elizabeth III. How had she managed to make herself the keeper of his conscience, or at least, his literary conscience?].

Jock fixed his eyes on the now empty table-cloth, the waiter having whisked everything away, and said, as though it had given him an idea:

'Now I've laid my cards on the table, sir, and I'm sorry for what's happened, but one thing led to another.'

Alexey, too, was sorry, and tried to get the various aspects of the situation into some kind of focus. But Pauline, the prime mover, wouldn't fit in. Now that his fantasy of her was shattered, she seemed just like any other woman, utterly outside the place in his imagination that she once held. With his mind, he was aware of the inconsistency of this, but not with his feelings.

'You shouldn't act too hastily,' he said. 'We don't know what view the law will take. Were the children fond of their mother?'

'I suppose they were, sir. Children often are. But they didn't have much time to know whether they were fond of her or not. Jean was only six, and Fergus was only three when she went off with this Jamaican.'

'Did you ever see him?' Alexey asked.

'No, sir. I was in bed and asleep when she slipped out, and I found she had left a note in pencil on the dressing-table, saying she had gone. She left a forwarding adddress for her things to be sent to, and I sent them and wrote to her, but I don't know if she got them, for she never answered.'

'She must have been slightly hard-hearted.'

'Oh, she was a tough girl, all right. Pretty, as you know, because you saw her. You shouldn't have seen her, and you wouldn't have seen her, if I had had my way, and if Miss Pauline hadn't been so headstrong. But women are like that, full of curiosity.'

'What did the Jamaican have that you haven't, Jock? More money, or what?'

Jock hesitated, and Alexey saw that after all these years he was still nursing a wound to his male pride.

'I wouldn't know what those wogs have, sir. People say they have something – in bed, I mean – that we white men don't have. They can –'

Jock's remark conjured up all sorts of possibilities, but Alexey didn't want to explore them.

'Now listen,' he said, 'we must be off if we want to be in London by bed-time, my bed-time. There's a room in my flat for you, as you know, so you needn't bother about sleeping out. But what I meant to say is this. You know my country cottage, near Oxford. You've been there more than once – with Miss Pauline. I haven't a chauffeur or a regular gardener, but I have a house-keeper, a middle-aged spinster who is fond of children. Why not stay with us, the three of you, until you find something you like better? I shall be lonely now, for a bit, and you would be company for me. Just think it over, and tell me on the way down, or tomorrow, or whenever you have made up your mind.'

'I will sir, I will,' said Jock, 'but first of all I must look at the car. There's a rattle in it that I don't quite like.' He jumped up, leaving the table-cloth creased and crumpled. 'I'll be back in a jiffy,' he said.

Have I been very stupid? Alexey asked himself. Have I saddled myself with three people, instead of one? And he remembered the parable of the empty heart, and the seven devils who entered it.

For a moment he succumbed to the feeling of vacancy that waiting for someone so often brings. Has Jock gone off somewhere? he wondered. Is he on his way to Gina, or Pauline?

But now Jock was standing in front of him, cap in hand, and like a railway-train, breathing the imminence of departure.

'It's nothing to worry about,' he said, 'just a small fault in the – but I dare say you wouldn't understand, sir.' There's a lot, thought Alexey, that I don't understand.

'Just a minute, please, sir, while I straighten my tie.' Jock went up to a large mirror and his face took on a look of extraordinary concentration, solemnity, even awe as he combed back his black hair. What store he sets by his appearance, thought Alexey, whose own tie had worked round to the right and was half hidden under his collar.

During the journey he dozed and woke up, and dozed again. In a moment of wakefulness he said.

'Did you think any more about my suggestion?'

'Your suggestion, sir?'

'Yes, about staying with me for the time being, to tide you over.'

'Oh yes,' said Jock, surprised. 'I thought you understood that I wanted to.'

'And what about Miss Pauline?'

'I think she can look after herself,' Jock said. 'She's had a good run for her money, hasn't she?'

'I suppose so,' said Alexey. 'I suppose so.' And for a moment the hang-over from his one-time intoxication with Pauline clouded his mind. 'What do you think she is doing now, Jock?'

'Oh, I couldn't say, sir. Looking round, you know, catching an eye here or there –'

'And you don't feel guilty about her?'

Jock didn't answer this question at once. He hadn't been reared a Presbyterian for nothing, and besides there was the traffic on the A.1 to overtake, or to be overtaken by. It was safer in the dark, as even Alexey knew, than in the twilight – like so many other things.

'No, sir, I don't, I don't feel guilty. She had her fun, didn't she?'

'Yes, but it's different with a woman.'

'If you'll excuse me, Mr. Alexey, I don't see that at all. To my way of thinking, women, women like her, women in the public eye, if you know what I mean, have all the best of it. They have men to trot them around, and boost them up, and give them a good opinion of themselves (which between you and I, is what they really want), and what do they give, in return for it?'

'They give a lot, Jock, they give a lot.'

'Only what they're paid to give. You know that, Mr. Alexey, as well as I do.'

'Perhaps we're exceptions,' Alexey said, 'perhaps we've been unlucky.'

For the second time in one day, for the second time in many years, Jock's face reddened. Although it was pitch dark in the car, and Alexey couldn't see the colour mounting in his cheeks, Jock felt aggrieved, and the more aggrieved because he didn't know why he was blushing. He had something to blush for, no doubt; but why at this particular moment? And he felt aggrieved, too (for he prided himself on his self-control) that the mechanism of blushing, which had lain dormant in him for many years and should have been obsolete by this time, had suddenly reasserted itself.

'We're just approaching Baldock now,' he said, for the sake of saying something. 'It won't matter much at this time of night, and being a Thursday, not a Friday, but it's a bottle-neck, as you know, sir, and it'll be a real god-send when they get that by-pass finished.'

'A bottle-neck?' said Alexey, surfacing from a semi-dream. 'Oh yes, all bottle-necks should be abolished – road-wise, I mean. Of course real bottles couldn't do without necks, could they?'

Jock laughed, indulgently.

What a stupid remark, thought Alexey, what am I coming to? I must be even more ga-ga than I thought I was. 'What I really meant,' he apologized, aloud, and untruthfully, 'is, that all the bottle-necks in our lives – you know what I mean, Jock – when we come into a traffic-block, going the opposite way or even the same way – they ought to be abolished.'

'Amen to that,' Jock said, fervently.

'And now,' said Alexey, restored to himself by this little excursion into symbolism, 'I'll tell you what I think we ought to do' [ought? yes ought, Elizabeth III and IV]. 'It depends on whether you agree of course.'

'I'm sure I shall agree,' said Jock, swerving to avoid an oncoming car.

'You shall see my solicitor in London tomorrow, and ask him what is the best course, whether to sue for a divorce from your wife on the grounds of desertion and adultery – you do want to divorce her, don't you?'

'Of course, I do, the bitch,' said Jock.

'Or to wait, until she sues you. The case, or rather the justice of the case, seems quite clear to me, but the law, I believe, tends to be on the side of the woman, and especially if she is a mother. Meanwhile, write to Mrs. Kirkwood, and thank her for her kindness to Jean and Fergus.'

'She was well paid for it,' interjected Jock.

'Yes, but let bygones be bygones. Ask her to send the children to my cottage – you know the address, anyhow here it is. Just stop a moment and turn the light on.' Alexey found a crumpled envelope in his pocket and scribbled on it.

'She won't do that without the money, sir. And besides the rail-fare there's the week's rent due in advance.'

Alexey frowned, but the frown was as invisible (except to Heaven) as Jock's blush had been.

'I know, we talked about that, but let's send her some money to cover it all. I can't bear to think of your dear children being victimized by their cruel playmates.'

'They're quite tough in their way,' said Jock, forgetting his earlier argument and defending his off-spring from the charge of timidity. 'They can hold their own against those Yorkshire brats.'

'Yes, but I'm sure it's better that they shouldn't have to. You remember the experience you had, when your school-mates pestered *you about your middle name. Now do be advised, Jock, and listen to what I say.'*

Jock didn't want to be advised by anyone. At the mere thought of it, a flame of opposition flared up in him. But he had been through a great deal; his financial position was precarious, and depended, for the moment, on Mr. Alexey's favour, to whom he owed so many favours. All this disposed him to take an objective view.

'Yes, sir, whatever you think best.'

They sped along the A.1, until the lights of London began to twinkle and thicken round them.

'I still keep thinking about Miss Pauline,' said Alexey suddenly (he always called her Miss Pauline to Jock). 'I still think about her and wonder if she is happy.' For all that Pauline meant to him as a person, he might have been thinking of Ariadne, deserted by Theseus, or Dido, abandoned by Aeneas.

'Do you think she is happy?' he asked again.

'Well, she wasn't when I last saw her,' said Jock, truthfully. 'She wasn't happy at all. I suppose she felt that the ground had given way under her. But doesn't this happen to all of us, at one time or another? I'm sure she can look after herself, I'm sure she can. She's a woman who will always attract men, for several years, at any rate. She's not like a film-star, anything but, but she makes enough to live on, without the etceteras, of course.'

Alexey thought that he had provided some of the etceteras, and that Jock had provided others. The latter was a thought he had always refused to entertain, for he couldn't believe in something he didn't want to believe in. All the same, how blessed is reassurance!

'She was never your mistress, was she, Jock?'

'No, sir,' said Jock promptly. 'Some people thought she was, just as they thought you was, sir, if you will excuse me for saying so.' He saw his mistake, and tried to correct it. 'Of course you couldn't have been her mistress – it wouldn't have been natural. But seeing as how we were all three so much mixed up, and the reporters, and so

on. But she never was, no, sir. She may have wanted to be' – he fixed his grip more firmly on the steering-wheel. 'But she never was.'

'I'm glad to hear you say so, Jock,' replied Alexey. 'In some way, I don't quite know how, it makes it better for all of us, doesn't it?'

Jock drove on without answering.

CHAPTER XIII

'Well, dearest Elizabeth, this is how the story ends. You said you were puzzled by the ending, by which I think you meant you would like me to say with which of the characters my sympathies lay.

Compassion! Compassion! I'm not sure that I felt very sorry for any of them, and I judge from the tone of your letter, that you didn't, either. They tried to fight their way out of Dante's *selva oscura*, the dark jungle in which they had lost their way, and from which they didn't emerge with much credit. Alexey was the luckiest, because besides having money, he had the capacity to live, emotionally, in a world of fantasy which kept the real world at bay. He suffered, when he lost Pauline, just as we all suffer when something dear to us is taken from us, either for their fault or ours; but not in the way *I* should suffer, dearest Elizabeth, if *you* were taken from me, because to me you are a person, as well as an ideal, not just the illusive Dulcinea, who obsessed (and inspired) Don Quixote.

To me, a novel, and the characters who compose it, make a synthesis of three points of view. One is what the novelist *wants* to happen; the second is what he or she thinks the reader would *like* to happen; and the third is what might *really* happen, in the light of common day, regarded objectively and without *parti pris*.

How hard it is to find a formula for this synthesis! I, as the author, should have liked everything to end happily but obviously it couldn't: so foul a sky clears not without a storm.

My readers, if any, may take sides with this character or with that. Pauline is to be pitied, Alexey is to be pitied, Jock is to be pitied, the children are to be pitied, Mrs. Kirkwood (little as she would have relished it) is to be pitied – but not Gina. I have thrown Gina to the wolves!

Pity, perhaps, but not liking. That is for you to judge. Liking, in my idea, demands a certain amount of moral approval, and I can't claim this for any of my characters; they are, or are meant to be, unregenerate children of their age.

And what would really have happened? This is a question that every serious novelist must always ask himself. Not what I want, nor what *you* want – dear Reader – but what the powers on high have decreed from the beginning of the world, without regard to our likes and dislikes.

I should have liked to find Pauline another protector, less exacting than Alexey but just as generous: I should have liked Jock and his children to settle down with Alexey, and having utterly defeated, in the law-court, the preposterous claims of his wife, Gina, to develop an *amitié amoureuse* with the house-keeper, which Alexey, of course, would never have noticed, but which *might* end in marriage.

And now may I tell you what I think *might* have happened? Alexey, having disposed of Pauline (we must remember, in Alexey's defence, that he no longer thought of Pauline as the woman he was in love with) – Alexey was fortunate in being able to transfer his affections to Jock & Co. He also felt he was doing good and adding to the sum of human happiness. It is more invigorating, if not always more praise-worthy, to start something new than to give up something old.

How Jock fared I have no idea. Better than Pauline, perhaps, for he was a down-to-earth character to whom security and the security money brings came first, though his children came a good second. Whereas Pauline, who depended upon money too, also depended on its intangible outgoings and incomings.

The Austin Princess at the kerb-side, and the handsome chauffeur in livery holding the door open, meant a great deal to her materially, but symbolically they meant still more; symbolically they were vital to any actress, or almost any actress, if she is to keep up the image, or the mirage of herself, whereon her success with the public is liable to depend. And losing Alexey she also lost Jock, who in one sense meant more to her than her career on the stage.

So my sympathies are really with Pauline, who had to put up with the loving longings, in season and out of season, of a man she didn't really care for, whose presence often irked her, and whose frequent letters, in his infrequent absences, she had to try to answer. How guilty she must have felt, and how bored! Sitting in the empty room, into which the voice of love was insistently pouring – as from a radio-set – with no inclination or ability on her part, to respond or even to listen!

On second thought, dearest Elizabeth, I won't try to tackle the 'reservations' you spoke of, for I don't want to be an Alexey to you, but I am and always shall be,

Your loving
James

In due course *The Love-Adept* came out. It had a mixed reception from the reviewers, not sufficiently favourable to warm the cockles of the author's heart, nor discouraging enough to freeze them. His publishers did what they could for it, and the public responded fairly well. Alas, they, the public, no longer wanted imaginative transcripts of everyday life, they wanted something further from it – science fiction – or close to it – biography. Facts, facts! The purveyors of science fiction could turn facts into fantasy, or fantasy into facts, which many people welcomed as an escape from the boredom of humdrum living. Or, if readers wanted facts near the knuckle, nude facts, historians and biographers could supply them. To know or not to know? The intermediate state, the twilight of the imagination, didn't attract them. No compromise between the old dispensation and the new!

On James, the publication of *The Love-Adept* had an effect which he hadn't anticipated. He rather prided himself on his ability to look into the future, and foresee Fate's next move. But he hadn't reckoned on this one. It was concerned with *The Love-Adept*, but only indirectly; it had little to do with the merits, or demerits of the story: it had to do with him.

Afterwards, he blamed himself for not having guessed what was bound to happen. Any novelist, any writer could have guessed it; but being obsessed, as most writers are, with the work in hand, he hadn't considered its possible, indeed its probable, side-effects on him.

Nor did he at once consciously realize what they were. He was aware of a change in himself, but, he told himself, such changes are inevitable as one grows older. One doesn't have the same reactions to oneself or to other people at the age of forty-five as one had at the age of twenty-five. It would be silly to expect to. James believed he was quite reasonable in such matters. There was a time when he enjoyed a ten-mile walk; now a five-mile walk was all, and rather more than all that he could manage. Never mind, he told himself, it's just that I'm getting older.

But the subconscious mind doesn't always, as we know, submit itself to the dictates of reason. Like the heart, it has its reasons, which reason knows not of; and when James found himself unwilling to go to parties to which he had been invited, he began to ask himself, 'Why? Why don't I want to go?'

Reason told him it was not because of his age; many men, and many women for that matter, older than he was, went quite gladly to parties – the sort of parties he was sometimes asked to, parties which he himself sometimes gave, though not as often as he should have, parties for his literary colleagues, cocktail parties for the most part, but sometimes wine-drinking parties in the evening.

He himself had once been an eager party-goer, and he still had invitations. The only partial success (or failure) of *The Love-Adept* hadn't diminished them; but he found he didn't want to go, and was always trumping up excuses for not going. Why? Was it because he was becoming anti-social, or a-social, or whatever the current term was? Was it because he didn't want to meet his colleagues in the literary field whom he had always enjoyed meeting? Or was it due to a middle-age spread – or a middle-age shrinkage?

No, it was suddenly borne in on him, it's because I am afraid of meeting the Elizabeths, even Elizabeth IV – to whom I so foolishly dedicated my book. At any party, one, two, three or all four of the Elizabeths may be present, and I dare not face them.

Why did I ever, he asked himself, tell the first three that I hadn't dedicated the book to them? It was a gesture of truth-telling (for James was morbidly truthful) but was it really necessary, any more than in war-time a journey was really necessary?

No, it wasn't. 'To Elizabeth' would have been quite enough – and they could have sorted it out for themselves, which Elizabeth he had meant, if they wanted to. Of course, he couldn't have guessed that each of the Elizabeths would have assumed he meant the book for her. What more insulting than to say, 'I'm sorry, it wasn't dedicated to you, it was dedicated to someone of the same name?' Tastelessness and tactlessness could go no further. Far better to have inscribed the book 'To Elizabeth, with hatred!' Then they would have known where they were, and where he was. The compromise, the ambiguity that had seemed so ingenious at the time – face-saving for everyone, including himself – now seemed a hideous mistake.

No, he couldn't bring himself to face them, singly or still worse, together.

It is a truism, but it cannot be too often repeated, that a bad habit is easier to acquire, as well as harder to break, than a good one. Indeed a good habit is one of the most fragile things in the world. Like friendship, it must be kept in constant repair. Whereas a bad habit will flourish like the green-bay tree, without any effort on the habitué's part to foster it.

Whenever James refused an invitation with the words 'Mr. James Golightly thanks Lady or Mrs. or Miss or Mr. so-and-so very much for her or his invitation for July 14th (it might be), 'and regrets that he is unable to accept it,' – he thought to himself 'What *am* I coming to? Soon I shan't be able to take a train, then I shan't be able to go out into the street' (he remembered the warning in the Book of Proverbs, 'The slothful man saith, "There is a lion without, I shall be slain in the streets"') then he would not dare to leave his sitting-room, then his bedroom, and then his bed. After that there would be no further withdrawal, except to the coffin, and the grave.

I really must snap out of this, he thought, as the drunkard thinks, when he refills his glass, 'or else I shall become my own prisoner, if not mine own executioner.'

At last the day came, the time and the place and the hostess (not called Elizabeth) all together, when the self-dissatisfaction and the self-criticism, which most writers and others experience, had been at work in him too long to be resisted. So against all his inclinations, he took up his pen and almost automatically, and as if another hand was guiding it, he wrote, 'Mr. James – thanks Mrs. – very much for her invitation and is delighted to accept it.'

Having committed himself, he suffered agonies. In vain he struggled with his over-active conscience, which always seemed to be arraigned against him. 'I can always get out of it,' he told himself. 'I can easily say that I am not well, or that I have been summoned to the bedside of a sick friend, or that I have had unexpectedly to go abroad.'

But his conscience would not let him. Being an off-shoot of the artist's conscience it would accept no excuses, and told him by day and by night, 'You have made your own bed, now you must lie on it.' But as the day of reckoning drew nigh, so did his tremors increase. 'If any of the Elizabeths are there,' (the voice of commonsense told him) 'which they almost certainly won't be, except possibly Elizabeth IV, Elizabeth Prescott, and you're not afraid of meeting her, are you? – you can just go into another part of the room, giving them a slightly evasive smile, and then carry on as one does carry on at a cocktail-party. You will find *someone* to talk to. What could be easier? In any case the noise will be so loud that your voice can't be heard, and if any Elizabeth comes up to you in a threatening manner, you can pretend not to see or hear her.'

All very well, but when you have incurred something – some obligation to yourself, or to your friends, or to society at large, it can't be shrugged off with a few well-chosen words, perhaps inaudible in the din of a cocktail-party.

.   .   .

'Have you seen anything of James lately?' asked Elizabeth I of Elizabeth II. 'I haven't, he doesn't seem to be in circulation.'

'Oh, but I thought he dedicated his last book to you. I can't remember what its title was. But surely you must have seen him.'

'Well, no, I haven't,' said Elizabeth II. 'After all, a *dédicace* isn't a passport to seeing someone, even if you like the book, which I didn't, specially. To tell you the truth, I thought he had dedicated *The Love-Adept* to *you*.'

The two women exchanged glances, and tried to get out of the way of other guests who were surging round them with backward looks of recognition, as much as to say, 'When you have a moment!'

'No,' said Elizabeth I, 'I wasn't sure, he didn't make it clear, which of us he meant it for. I thought he meant it for *you*. But does it really matter? If the book had been a masterpiece, which, alas, it isn't, then we might have been clawing each other's eyes out.'

They looked around them at the room, so brightly lit beneath its chandeliers, and at the other guests, all talking happily about books, and possibly about *The Love-Adept* which was still news.

'I'm genuinely surprised it wasn't you,' said Elizabeth I, 'it wasn't *me*, at least he never said so. How teasing men can be! Women are much more straightforward. If I had written a book – which I couldn't – I should have said, 'From Elizabeth to James,' – and no one would have been the wiser.'

'We aren't the wiser now,' said Elizabeth II. 'Isn't that just as well? But it was rather naughty of James, oughtn't he to have said who, or whom, he meant the book for?'

In their secret hearts they debated the question, and then Elizabeth II said, 'Look, I see another Elizabeth who used to be a friend of James's. Let's ask her.'

Together they converged upon a shortish, dark woman, with a gleaming, slightly aggressive eye, and cut off her retreat.

'Elizabeth!'

'Elizabeth!'

'Elizabeth!'

'Yes, I am Elizabeth,' said Elizabeth III, 'Isn't it an awful party? But now I've had the good luck to meet you –'

'We wanted to talk to you,' said Elizabeth II, 'about our great friend James, our mutual friend. He really has put the cat among the canaries, if we can describe ourselves – she included the other two Elizabeths in her glance – as canaries.'

'I have no idea what you are talking about,' said Elizabeth III. 'Cat, canaries? Which is which?'

'You wouldn't remember,' said Elizabeth II, who had made herself the spokeswoman, 'but James dedicated his last novel, *The Love-Adept*, to a certain Elizabeth, and we both thought that you must be she.'

'Then you were quite mistaken,' said Elizabeth III. 'I disliked the book intensely, and I told him so. I said, "If there is still time to delete the dedication (I had an advance copy) please do so," and he replied – I suppose sincerely – that I wasn't the

Elizabeth he had in mind. It was a snub, I dare say, but I don't mind being snubbed in a good cause.'

'But then who?' exclaimed the other Elizabeths in unison. 'It must have been *one* of us.'

'I am surprised you should want to claim such a doubtful privilege,' said Elizabeth III. 'He may have meant anyone, he may have meant Queen Elizabeth the First, in which case he would have had his head chopped off, and rightly, or he may have meant our present Queen, who wouldn't be flattered, either.'

'Shall we put a curse on the book?' said Elizabeth II. 'Not, I'm sure, that it needs a curse.' She looked at her co-Elizabeths. 'How many Elizabeths constitute a *coven*? When shall we three meet again, in thunder, lightning or in –'

At that moment they saw James, not exactly bearing down on them, but outflanking them, with Elizabeth IV not quite on his arm, but as near as might be.

'My dear Elizabeth!'

'My dear Elizabeth!'

'My dear Elizabeth!'

And then, in chorus from the three witches:

'My dear James!'

'Well,' said he, looking from face to face, 'this is a most happy occasion, isn't it? To find all my dear Elizabeths to-gether? And this one' (he gave Elizabeth IV's arm a tug) 'to swell the number? How happy I am to meet you all again, and how happy I hope you will be, to know that my long probation of singularity, I was going to say, but bachelorhood is what I mean – is over at last! Oh, my dear Elizabeths, I can't tell you what you have meant to me in the way of inspiration, happi-ness, *joie-de-vivre*, enhancement of life –'. He stopped, unable to say more. It hadn't crossed his mind, until the last moment, when his dread of possible encounters with the other Elizabeths became too great to be borne, that he had the idea of asking Elizabeth IV to accompany him to the cocktail-party; but to his astonishment she had said she would. She had been invited, but as is the manner of some people in these days she had forgotten to reply.

'We were talking about you,' said Elizabeth III, addressing herself to James, in her blunt way, 'and wondering why we hadn't seen you. Have you been in hiding from your last book, *The Love-Adept*? Were you afraid that we were all going to pounce on you? Alexey, the good-natured *squire de dames*?'

She glanced at her Elizabethan companions, who didn't know which way to look.

Elizabeth IV, too, seemed embarrassed, and clung tightly to James's arm.

'Don't bother about it, please don't bother about it,' he said. 'I mean you especially,' and he bowed to Elizabeth III. 'We're with our common friends – I won't say our mutual friends, because that is a grammatical mistake that even Dickens was guilty of – but' – and he took a glass of champagne from the waiter, 'we all love each other, don't we, Elizabeth, Elizabeth, Elizabeth?' And he raised his glass, but before raising it, he gave a sip to Elizabeth IV, who seemed to like it all the better for the touch of his lips.

The other Elizabeths drank their champagne in silence, and then Elizabeth II, the most vocal, and apart from Elizabeth III, the most outspoken, asked, 'Whom are we really toasting? Is it you James? Or is it you?' and she gave an affectionate wink to Elizabeth IV. 'Or is it Alexey and Pauline? Perhaps they will come together again, once Jock's out of the way.'

Her smile was tinged with malice; but Elizabeth III said, 'As far as I got in the book, James, which, as you know, wasn't very far, Jock was the only character I cared for.' She looked

175

round the room, but there was no one at all like Jock in sight. 'At any rate, he knew his own mind.'

'Oh, so you did finish the book?' exclaimed James.

'*Did* I say I finished it? I got as far as I could. Did *you* finish it?' she turned accusingly to Elizabeths I and II.

'Of course we did, how can you ask?' they demanded almost in chorus.

'I didn't know, but whichever of us is Pauline, I'm sorry for her. And now,' she said, looking at her Elizabethan companions one by one, until her dark eyes rested on Elizabeth IV, 'is this an ordinary cocktail-party, or is it in celebration of something or someone?'

'It is an ordinary cocktail-party,' said James, 'except for us, Elizabeth' – he gave Elizabeth IV a fond look – 'Elizabeth and me. For *us*,' he went on, amazed at his own boldness, 'it *is* a celebration.'

'A celebration of *what*, if I may ask?' said Elizabeth III.

James gave his Elizabeth an interrogative glance. Her slight nod, her lowered eyes and her lifted eyebrows, seemed to imply consent.

'It's in celebration of our engagement, if you really want to know.'

'Congratulations.'

'Congratulations.'

'Congratulations.'

They all seemed pleased; but Elizabeth III said, before they broke up to join the crowd, 'What an old deceiver you are! Alexey had nothing on you!'

'I thought, in fact you told me, that you had never been able to finish the book!' retorted James with unaccustomed spirit, and fortified by the presence of Elizabeth IV at his side.

'I only finished it,' said Elizabeth III, 'because you had dedicated it to me, and it seemed uncivil not to. You withdrew the dedication because I told you I didn't like the book, and the more I read it, the more I disliked it.'

Anger made her look smaller and darker, as she flashed her black eyes at the other Elizabeths.

'Oh, I think you are making a fuss about nothing,' said James, leaning towards her and clinking his glass with hers. 'There are so many Elizabeths – my mother was called Elizabeth, so was my aunt Lizzy, who was an expert in making paper-boats. How I loved them, when I was a child! Elizabeth is almost a generic name for someone I like!'

His glance appealed to them all for approval, but it was only Elizabeth IV who smiled.

'It never occurred to me,' said Elizabeth II, 'that James had dedicated *The Love-Adept* to me. I should never have presumed that I was on his dedicatory list.'

'Nor I,' said Elizabeth I. 'I thought it might be – well – so many of our friends – but not me, no, not me.'

'There I differ from you,' said Elizabeth III, 'I did think, and I still think, that James meant the book for me. Not that I wanted it, Heaven forbid! But if someone says 'Elizabeth'', I am conceited enough to imagine it means me.'

The party around them, unconscious of them, was growing mellower and mellower; it was Liberty Hall.

'Let's play ring-a-ring-a-roses,' said James, suddenly. They linked hands and danced a round or two, to the amusement of the onlookers, who drew back to make way for them. It was the Grand Parenthesis, but before they got as far as 'A-tishoo, A-tishoo, and we all fall down,' they realized how unsuitable such an action would be to people of their age; and if they fell down, how could they ever get up?

After this childish display, parting seemed quite easy, and hardly needed a good-bye.

'You did very well,' said Elizabeth IV as they waited on the pavement for a taxi. 'I'm proud of you. All those other Elizabeths, nice as they are –'

'We mustn't be hard on them,' said James, 'they have the vice of meaning well.'

He wasn't sure if they had, nor, as he and she embraced in the comfortable privacy of the taxi, did he tell his chosen Elizabeth that he would not have proposed marriage to her if he hadn't been afraid of meeting her namesakes, and with them, the strictures of the outside world.

'You said you didn't quite understand the ending of my story,' James said.

'What story?'

'*My* story.'

'*Your* story – oh, you mean *The Love-Adept*. You mean *that*?'

'Yes,' said James, a little abashed, but bearing up. 'Well, *this* is how it ends.'

He kissed her again.